BARELY SEEN

(A Tessa Flint FBI Suspense Thriller —Book 1)

Molly Black

Molly Black

Bestselling author Molly Black is author of the MAYA GRAY FBI suspense thriller series, comprising eleven books; of the RYLIE WOLF FBI suspense thriller series, comprising six books; of the TAYLOR SAGE FBI suspense thriller series, comprising eight books; of the KATIE WINTER FBI suspense thriller series, comprising eleven books (and counting); of the RUBY HUNTER FBI suspense thriller series, comprising five books (and counting); of the CAITLIN DARE FBI suspense thriller series, comprising six books (and counting); of the REESE LINK mystery series, comprising six books (and counting); of the CLAIRE KING FBI suspense thriller series, comprising seven books (and counting); of the PIPER WOODS mystery series, comprising six books (and counting); of the GRACE FORD mystery series, comprising seven books (and counting); of the CASEY BOLT mystery series, comprising five books (and counting); of the JADE SAVAGE mystery series, comprising five books (and counting); of the TESSA FLINT mystery series, comprising seven books (and counting); of the CLARA PIKE FBI thriller series, comprising five books (and counting); and of the ELISE CLOSE psychological thriller series, comprising five books (and counting).

An avid reader and lifelong fan of the mystery and thriller genres, Molly loves to hear from you, so please feel free to visit www.mollyblackauthor.com to learn more and stay in touch.

ISBN: 978-1-0943-9703-0

BOOKS BY MOLLY BLACK

ELISE CLOSE MYSTERY SERIES
BEHIND HER LIES (Book #1)
BEHIND HER SMILE (Book #2)
BEHIND HER SECRETS (Book #3)
BEHIND HER GATES (Book #4)
BEHIND LOCKED DOORS (Book #5)

CLARA PIKE FBI SUSPENSE THRILLER SERIES
REMEMBER THE FEAR (Book #1)
REMEMBER THE DEAD (Book #2)
REMEMBER THE LIES (Book #3)
REMEMBER THE SILENCE (Book #4)
REMEMBER THE PAST (Book #5)

PIPER WOODS FBI SUSPENSE THRILLER
SOMEWHERE SAFE (Book #1)
SOMEWHERE SANE (Book #2)
SOMEWHERE WHOLE (Book #3)
SOMEWHERE FAR (Book #4)
SOMEWHERE WRONG (Book #5)
SOMEWHERE HIDDEN (Book #6)

TESSA FLINT MYSTERY SERIES
BARELY SEEN (Book #1)
BARELY HEARD (Book #2)
BARELY FORGOTTEN (Book #3)
BARELY MISSING (Book #4)
BARELY ALIVE (Book #5)
BARELY THERE (Book #6)
BARELY SILENT (Book #7)

CASEY BOLT MYSTERY SERIES
BROKEN (Book #1)
FLAWED (Book #2)
BLEMISHED (Book #3)

DAMAGED (Book #4)
TWISTED (Book #5)

GRACE FORD MYSTERY SERIES
NEARLY MINE (Book #1)
NEARLY SAFE (Book #2)
NEARLY FREE (Book #3)
NEARLY GONE (Book #4)
NEARLY HIS (Book #5)

CLAIRE KING MYSTERY SERIES
ONCE HE SEES (Book #1)
ONCE HE LONGS (Book #2)
ONCE HE TAKES (Book #3)
ONCE HE FEELS (Book #4)
ONCE HE KNOWS (Book #5)

MAYA GRAY MYSTERY SERIES
GIRL ONE: MURDER (Book #1)
GIRL TWO: TAKEN (Book #2)
GIRL THREE: TRAPPED (Book #3)
GIRL FOUR: LURED (Book #4)
GIRL FIVE: BOUND (Book #5)
GIRL SIX: FORSAKEN (Book #6)
GIRL SEVEN: CRAVED (Book #7)
GIRL EIGHT: HUNTED (Book #8)
GIRL NINE: GONE (Book #9)
GIRL TEN: WANTED (Book #10)
GIRL ELEVEN: VANISHED (Book #11)

RYLIE WOLF FBI SUSPENSE THRILLER SERIES
FOUND YOU (Book #1)
CAUGHT YOU (Book #2)
SEE YOU (Book #3)
WANT YOU (Book #4)
TAKE YOU (Book #5)
DARE YOU (Book #6)

TAYLOR SAGE FBI SUSPENSE THRILLER SERIES
DON'T LOOK (Book #1)

DON'T BREATHE (Book #2)
DON'T RUN (Book #3)
DON'T FLINCH (Book #4)
DON'T REMEMBER (Book #5)
DON'T TELL (Book #6)

KATIE WINTER FBI SUSPENSE THRILLER SERIES
SAVE ME (Book #1)
REACH ME (Book #2)
HIDE ME (Book #3)
BELIEVE ME (Book #4)
HELP ME (Book #5)
FORGET ME (Book #6)
HOLD ME (Book #7)
PROTECT ME (Book #8)
REMEMBER ME (Book #9)
CATCH ME (Book #10)
WATCH ME (Book #11)

RUBY HUNTER FBI SUSPENSE THRILLER SERIES
IF I RUN (Book #1)
IF I TELL (Book #2)
IF I LIVE (Book #3)
IF I FORGET (Book #4)
IF I RETURN (Book #5)

CAITLIN DARE FBI SUSPENSE THRILLER SERIES
COME GET ME (Book #1)
COME FIND ME (Book #2)
COME TAKE ME (Book #3)
COME CATCH ME (Book #4)
COME SAVE ME (Book #5)

REESE LINK MYSTERY SERIES
BEYOND REASON (Book #1)
BEYOND REACH (Book #2)
BEYOND REPAIR (Book #3)
BEYOND DOUBT (Book #4)
BEYOND NORMAL (Book #5)

PROLOGUE

The chandeliers sprinkled light like stardust across the grand foyer, reflecting off the polished marble floors and illuminating the opulent interior of Mary's sprawling estate. She was a vision of wealth as she sauntered through her home, the queen of her domain, overseeing the final preparations for what promised to be the social event of the season.

"Everything must be perfect," she murmured to herself, her voice echoing slightly in the cavernous space. Caterers moved all around the room with precision, setting silver cutlery atop white linen tablecloths with practiced hands while the florist arranged roses and lilies into artful displays.

Mary ascended the sweeping staircase, the hem of her silk gown whispering against the steps. In her bedroom, she approached the full-length mirror and paused, taking in her reflection. The dress clung to her figure in all the right places, the deep emerald color complementing her auburn hair, which was styled in a sophisticated chignon.

"Simply divine," she whispered, allowing herself a small, satisfied smile. Mary reached for her necklace, a string of perfectly matched pearls that had been in her family for generations. As she fastened the clasp and adjusted the strand so it lay just so against her collarbone, a strange noise from downstairs interrupted her reverie.

It was a sound out of place amid the quiet clinking of glassware and subdued chatter of the staff — a subtle scraping, like something being dragged across wood. Her brow furrowed in momentary confusion. Was it the new butler? He seemed competent enough, but everyone required a period of adjustment in her household. Was the idiot sliding something heavy across her floors?

"Probably nothing," she rationalized internally, but curiosity gnawed at her like a persistent moth. Mary wasn't one to ignore her intuition, a trait that had helped her navigate the treacherous waters of high society with aplomb. And even if it was the new butler, maybe he needed a good talking to.

With a last glance in the mirror, she resolved to investigate the disturbance herself. After all, a hostess could never be too vigilant on the eve of such an important affair. It would not do to have any mishaps. Mary descended the staircase, the soft rustle of her gown barely audible over the burgeoning sensation of unease that tinged the edges of her thoughts.

"Surely, it's just the wind," she told herself, even as her hand tightened imperceptibly around the pearl at her throat.

Back downstairs, she passed through the thrum of activity in the foyer as preparations were coming to a close. She made her way to the grand living room, perfumed with the scent of freshly cut lilies and the subtle undertone of beeswax from the polished antique furniture. Mary stepped into the space, her every sense heightened to a keen edge. The sound that had drawn her back downstairs was not repeated, yet the silence that followed seemed to thrum with expectancy.

"Is someone there?" Her voice, normally commanding and assured, wavered slightly as it echoed off the high ceilings adorned with intricate moldings.

No response came, just the murmur of movement and voices from the foyer. But as her eyes adjusted to the dim light – the chandeliers purposely dimmed before guests arrived to create an atmosphere of intimacy – she saw him. A figure, male in silhouette, stood perfectly still by the grand piano. His hand was outstretched, a string of pearls hanging like captured moonlight between his fingers. She didn't recognize him, which wasn't saying much, seeing how she had hired over twenty people to make sure tonight went off without a hitch.

"Who are you?" she demanded, the grip on her own necklace tightening instinctively. "What do you want?"

He said nothing. Instead, he took a step towards her, deliberate and unhurried. Mary's heart pounded in her chest, a wild rhythm that felt at odds with the calmness of the intruder's approach. Each step he took seemed measured; a predator confident in its pursuit.

As he neared, the moonlight streaming through the French windows caught on something metallic in his hand – a syringe. Panic surged within Mary's chest, but years of maintaining composure under scrutiny held her in place. This must be some kind of misunderstanding, she thought desperately.

"Stay back!" Her command was firm, but the man did not heed. He was close now, close enough that she could see the chilling emptiness in his eyes.

"Beautiful pearls for a beautiful lady," he murmured, his voice disturbingly serene.

"Get away from me!"

But it was too late. With a sudden movement, he grabbed her arm, and the needle pierced her skin, cold as ice. Pain exploded through her body, immediate and debilitating. It radiated from the injection site, seizing her muscles with merciless ferocity. Her legs buckled beneath her, and she fell to her knees, the plush carpet doing little to cushion the blow.

Her mind raced, thoughts fragmenting under the onslaught of agony. This can't be happening. Who is he? Why can't I move? Perhaps someone from the foyer heard me speaking to him and would come to help.

Mary's vision began to blur at the edges, the glittering surfaces and rich textures of the room morphing into a swirl of indistinct shapes and shadows. She wanted to cry out, to demand help, but the pain was a vice around her lungs, squeezing the breath from her body in silent gasps.

"Shh," the man whispered, as if consoling a child. "Don't fight it. Just let go."

She couldn't let go. Not here. Not like this. But her body betrayed her, succumbing to whatever she'd been injected with as her world narrowed to a pinpoint of light in a sea of encroaching darkness.

Mary's throat constricted. The scream she intended to unleash was trapped behind the vice-like grip of agony that throttled her voice. Her mouth opened in a silent cry, a wordless plea for mercy, but only the shallow, ragged breaths of suffocating terror emerged. The pain was an entity unto itself, a beast with claws sunk deep into her flesh, shredding any semblance of control. She clawed at her neck, fingers trembling, trying to alleviate the invisible stranglehold.

"Ah, such a shame," the intruder cooed, his tone a macabre lullaby in the midst of chaos. "Pearls should never witness such ugliness, don't you think?" He advanced, the soft click of his shoes on the marble floor a sinister metronome to Mary's erratic heartbeat.

Her panicked eyes locked onto the string of pearls in his hand – identical to the one encircling her own throat. A gift from her late husband, those pearls had graced countless galas, shimmering under chandeliers as testimony to her status. Now, they were an instrument of her demise.

"Let me adjust this for you." His fingers were cold and precise, grazing her skin as he lifted the necklace, giving the pearls a gentle twist. They tightened a constrictor's coil, pressing into her flesh with an intimacy that made her stomach churn.

Mary's thoughts splintered like glass under the weight of the realization that these could be her final moments. Each labored breath was a battle, each tick of the clock a step closer to her end. What would they say about her? Would they remember her charity work, her soirées, or just the tragic end that befell her?

"Perfect," he whispered, admiring his handiwork. "Pearls are the queens of gems and the gem of queens. And tonight, you are regal."

The irony of his words cut through the fog of pain. She was no queen, merely prey in her own home, a castle-turned-trap. As the room spun, Mary grappled with despair, the gilded edges of her life blurring into a nightmare she could not escape. The last thing she saw before darkness nipped at her consciousness was the glint of the pearls, now a noose rather than a necklace – a symbol of luxury turned lethal.

As the killer's monologue droned on, Mary's once vibrant world shrank to the size of the room – a mausoleum of her former glories adorned with crystal chandeliers and silk drapes that now witnessed her pain. Her muscles screamed in silent protest against the toxin coursing through her veins, rendering her a living statue amidst her own opulence.

"Strength, my dear," he cooed, his voice a velvet caress against the horror of his actions. "The strength of pearls lies in their layers. Layer upon layer, they build themselves up against irritation. You've built up your life in much the same way, haven't you? But unlike these little miracles of nature, you seem to have lost your luster."

His words twisted in her mind, knotting with the agony that bound her limbs. She wanted to rage, to berate him for his audacity, but she could only muster a gaze filled with defiance that he seemed to drink in like a connoisseur savoring a fine wine.

With deliberate slowness, the killer turned from her and moved to the ornate bar cart that rested by the window, its contents untouched and awaiting celebration. He picked up an unopened bottle of champagne, the label a testament to years aged to perfection – a stark contrast to the premature ending being scripted for her.

"Ah, this will do nicely," he murmured as the pop of the cork echoed through the room like the starting shot of some macabre race she would not finish.

Mary watched helplessly as he tilted the bottle, liquid gold cascading into two fluted glasses with a celebratory bubble and fizz. The familiar sound, once a herald of joy and laughter, now played a requiem for her spirit, which seemed to flicker and wane with each passing second.

"Every memorable event deserves a toast, wouldn't you agree?" he asked rhetorically, turning back to her with one glass in his hand, the other offered as if she could reach out and accept it. His smile was a grotesque parody of geniality. "To life's final luxuries."

As he lifted the glass to his lips, Mary felt the darkness creep closer, wrapping around her consciousness with the inevitability of nightfall. Each sip he took was a countdown to oblivion.

"Such fragile things, pearls," the killer mused aloud, his voice a soft caress that belied the sharpness of his actions. "Born from discomfort, layer upon layer, until they emerge into the world—a perfect product of agitation."

Mary's vision began to waver, her eyes struggling to focus on the gleaming string of pearls in the killer's hand. Her body was betraying her, collapsing inward as the toxin spread its roots through her veins.

"Isn't it poetic?" he continued, oblivious or indifferent to her distress. "You adorned yourself with these little emblems of adversity, yet you never expected to become one yourself."

Her breath came in shallow gasps, and she fought for air as if surfacing from the depths of a murky sea. Her hand instinctively rose, fingers trembling as they clutched at the unique pearl that dangled just above her heart—an oddity among the uniformity, much like herself in the elite circles she once navigated with such ease.

"Your vision is dimming," he observed, his tone almost clinical. "The end approaches, Mary. But fear not; your beauty will remain intact, frozen in time. You'll be an everlasting monument to purity... well, the illusion of it."

As her senses dulled, the room was no longer a dimming pinprick; it suddenly seemed to stretch and distort around her. The grandeur of her surroundings faded into a hazy backdrop for this surreal finale.

"Sleep now," he whispered, lifting his glass in a silent salute to her faltering form.

A profound coldness enveloped her, seeping into her bones as the last vestiges of warmth fled her body. It was then that the lights flickered—a prelude to darkness—and Mary's world dissolved into shadow.

CHAPTER ONE

Tessa Flint's muscles were coiled springs, her focus like a laser as she stood at the starting line of the FBI's notorious obstacle course. The air was thick with the scent of rubber, dirt, and sweat, an ambiance that would unnerve many. But not Tessa. To her, it was the perfume of challenge, luring her toward the challenge.

She looked over to the instructor, waiting. Her vision wasn't even taking in the others huddled around the sidelines. In that moment, it was just her and the instructors.

"Go!" barked the instructor, and she launched forward like a bullet from a gun.

She sprinted forward, her legs like a machine. Everything to her left and right was nothing more than blurs of color and motion.

"Look at her go," someone murmured from the sidelines. The words barely reached Tessa's ears over the thud of her own boots hammering the ground. She vaulted over hurdles with the grace of a gazelle, each landing precise, her body obeying her iron will without question.

"Damn, she's making us look bad," another voice said, tinged with respect and a hint of envy. But the chatter of her colleagues faded into white noise, her entire world narrowing to the obstacles before her.

The intricate network of ropes loomed ahead, a tangle designed to entangle and exhaust. But exhaustion was a language Tessa didn't speak. There were many things about her body that were unique—namely the fact that she'd been born with a rare inability to feel pain, turned what would be a grueling trial for others into merely a complex puzzle for her extraordinary physique.

Tessa attacked the ropes, climbing with such fluidity and speed it seemed as though she were part spider. A lesser agent might have hesitated, muscles burning, skin chafing raw against the coarse fibers, but Tessa felt none of it. Instead, her mind was clear, focused solely on the ascent, her body moving without the distraction of discomfort or the threat of injury.

"Unbelievable," an older agent muttered, shaking his head. "I've run this course hundreds of times. Never seen anything like it."

As Tessa reached the summit of the rope structure, she paused only to assess her descent. The others on the scene were still nothing more than background shapes. She had a task ahead of her, and that was all that mattered. Fast, efficient, and silent, she rappelled down, hitting the ground in a roll that absorbed her momentum and propelled her toward the next hurdle.

"Every damn time," the instructor grumbled, though there was no mistaking the undercurrent of pride in his tone.

Tessa didn't respond, didn't even smile. There was no room for pride, only purpose. This was her playground, and every inch of the course she dominated was another step towards readiness, towards being unbreakable in the face of whatever twisted puzzles awaited her in the field.

Her breath came steady, unaffected by exertion, as she approached the final wall—a towering monolith that had tested the limits of countless agents. Without a flicker of hesitation, Tessa scaled it, her fingers finding holds invisible to most, her body leveraging upwards with mechanical precision.

Distantly, she became aware of a small bit of blood on one of the lengths of rope along the wall. She took half a second to look at the palm side of her hand. A blister between her ring and middle fingers had burst open. She, of course, hadn't felt it. Not the tear of the skin, not the sting along her hand as she continued to use the hand to conquer the course.

This was nothing new to her. She'd gather little scrapes and cuts here or there and not notice them until she was in the shower or undressing. Sometimes, she'd find large bruises with no idea where they'd come from.

Her thoughts retreated to a memory triggered by the challenge—the concern etched on her parents' faces as they discussed her condition in hushed tones. *You're special,* they'd told her. *Maybe in more ways than we could have ever guessed.* These memories often came out of nowhere. She supposed it was because she'd spent so long suppressing them. One of the therapists she'd seen as a teen had warned her that trauma finds a way out if it isn't properly processed. She supposed that's what was occurring whenever the memories from her past presented themselves in the most unlikely of moments.

To some, the idea of the inability to feel pain was amazing—almost a blessing. But Tessa had lived with it all her life, a bizarre medical condition that had kept doctors stumped all throughout her childhood.

She lived with the fear that she could get a minor cut and not know it, risking a major infection.

But for now, it was just an annoying, popped blister. She'd live. And besides…she had records to smash.

"Time!" the instructor called out.

Tess leaped from the top and landed catlike on the other side. The timer beeped, a digital herald confirming what all present already knew—Tessa Flint was in a league of her own.

"Flint, if I didn't see it with my own eyes every time..." the instructor started, offering a nod that conveyed a cocktail of admiration and disbelief.

Tessa simply collected her water bottle, her chest barely rising and falling despite the feat. She didn't need their awe; she needed results, needed to be sharper, faster, stronger. Because out there, beyond the safety of training grounds, lay real monsters, and she intended to be their most formidable nightmare. It was something she'd set her sights on at a young age, a goal that had never changed or faltered.

As she drank down some water, her instructor came over. He was smiling in disbelief, an expression that seemed odd on his usually stone-like face.

"Damn good work, Flint."

"Thanks, sir."

"You should know that I just got word just before your run that Lawson needs to see you. Conference Room B."

"Yes, sir."

She didn't even hesitate a single moment. She turned away from the obstacle course and started down the wide dirt trail that led back to the field office. Sweating and with a nice, steady heartbeat, Tessa put the obstacle course behind her and headed for the conference room, where she was sure she'd be confronted with an entirely different sort of puzzle.

CHAPTER TWO

With the day's victory behind her, Tessa found herself beneath the harsh glare of fluorescent lights at the gym. She preferred boxing-style workouts, though there were days when she branched out to activities like simple weights or when she was feeling in need of a reset, even yoga.

But today, she felt the need for exertion, to throw some punches. Each strike against the punching bag was a silent conversation with her own body—a body that had never known the sting of pain yet moved with such lethal grace. When the skin of her knuckles peeled back, she didn't feel the sting of it. When she struck a bit too hard for the comfort of her wrist, she wasn't aware of her body's protests.

Another reason she felt the need to box today was because the memories of her sister had been stronger than ever as of late. Sarah…Sarah's cold case. Sarah's disappearance.

It had been nearly ten years now, and her sister's disappearance still haunted her as much as it had during the days following the event.

She saw Sarah's smiling face, taken from her and her father—and she punched. She saw the screen window pulled from the frame of Sara's room—and she jabbed. She saw the perplexed and waxen faces of every single policeman who had come around, and she punched harder.

One of those faces had been that of her father. And when *that* memory popped up, Tessa punched as hard as she could. She did not feel the pain of the punches in her hands or wrists, but she could feel the sweat and the stickiness of blood from peeled knuckles. And when she was done, feeling like she'd properly exorcised her demons for the moment, she moved on.

She transitioned from blows to weights, muscles contracting rhythmically. Iron plates clinked, a metallic symphony. This was where she honed not just her strength but her resolve, steeling herself for battles to come. As a federal agent with a special skillset and ability, she could never be sure what sort of enemy she'd come up against next. It was always smart to be prepared.

From punching bags to weights, then to the gym showers, she felt her day unspool predictably. She had no qualms with predictability…not really. She rather enjoyed knowing every next step; it was a counterweight to the unpredictability of her condition and how the memories of her past had suddenly started to assault her out of the blue.

She left the gym and wound her way through Portland. It was about half an hour's drive, but she enjoyed it, especially at this time of day, just before the night had properly fallen. Her home was a simple little beach house by the coast, passed down by her grandmother. For whatever reason, her father had declined it and passed it on to her when she'd come home from Quantico—the one redeeming thing, in her eyes, the man had ever done in the span of years following her mother's suicide.

There, with the sound of the crashing waves against the Maine coast, Tessa surrounded herself with books and screens of text. Physics theories entwined with the psychology of deviance, languages both computer and foreign, splayed open before her. She was currently reading a hardback copy of a physics textbook, but when she got up to make herself a cup of chamomile tea, she switched to an audiobook on the nature of evil.

Her living room was a study in shadows, bathed in the pale blue hue of evening sky filtering through the blinds. And evening light, in her eyes, was always made a bit more beautiful when it was this close to the sea. Tessa sat cross-legged on her couch, sipping on her tea and thinking of the half-eaten salad waiting for her in the fridge—which would likely end up being her dinner. As dusk approached, she stood up from the couch and stared out the window. The ocean was just barely visible, hidden away by rocky terrain and meager dunes, but she could see the white caps of several waves forming and inching toward the coast.

She picked up a framed photograph from the end table, a captured moment of a young girl with two beaming parents. Her fingertips traced the glass, but it was as if she were touching a life that belonged to someone else.

She set the frame down and closed her eyes. Her mind roamed corridors that others shied away from, craving connection, yet unable to fully grasp it. With her condition, pain was an abstract concept, and without it, so was much of the human experience.

Tessa's moment of quiet was shattered by the piercing ring of her cell phone. She snatched it up from the coffee table, recognizing the number instantly. It was Special Agent in Charge Rebecca Lawson. And she only ever called her cellphone after business hours if it was something important—something involving a case.

"This is Flint," she answered sharply. She felt a spike of excitement and adrenaline, her body getting ready for whatever was to come.

"We've got a dead body, Flint," Lawsons said, cutting straight to the chase. "Looks like the same M.O. as the Rogers case. And if that is indeed the case, it looks like we've got a serial on our hands."

Tessa's eyes sharpened, the analyst in her already dissecting the implications. The first victim, a pearl necklace constricting her breath, the killer's fixation clear. "Same M.O.?" she said. "Pearls?"

"Yeah. Unmistakable."

Pearls and pain, Tessa thought. *A weird combination indeed.*

"Where?" was all she asked, mentally cataloging the evidence from the first victim, Mrs. Mary Rogers. Injected with something. Pearls. Slow asphyxiation. And now there was another.

"Portland. 47 Westbury Lane," Lawson responded. "You need to see this for yourself, Flint. We're dealing with a sophisticated predator. And Agent Sullivan has already been notified. He's currently on the way over there."

"Understood." Tessa's voice was calm, her demeanor collected. She ended the call and grabbed her leather jacket, slipping it over her shoulders. She paused for a second, glancing back at the photograph on the table. Her parents' smiles seemed to urge her on, to chase the darkness that others couldn't face.

With the call ended, leaving Tessa wrapped in silence once more. She slipped into her tactical boots, their scuff marks testament to past pursuits, and holstered her weapon with practiced ease. Her movements were swift, decisive; there was no room for hesitation in the world she navigated.

As she locked her door behind her, her mind churned with the scarce details provided. A second victim, a serial killer's signature marked by pearls and pain—pain that would have been excruciating for anyone who could feel it. But Tessa's own condition made her immune to such agony, a fact that both isolated and empowered her.

Her stride was purposeful as she walked down the porch steps toward her car. The night air greeted her with a slight sea-tinged chill. Tessa welcomed it, let it fill her lungs and clear her thoughts. The killer was out there, cloaked in darkness, but Tessa was on the hunt—and she had never been one to shy away from the shadows.

***

The scent of copper and tragedy hung heavily in the air as Tessa crossed the threshold into the parlor where the second victim had met her grisly fate. The room, a shrine to affluence with its grandiose artworks and plush furnishings, now bore the macabre signature of murder. Tessa's eyes, honed by years of parsing scenes just like this one, began their meticulous dance—scanning, cataloging, searching for the silent witnesses that spoke in whispers only she could interpret.

Upon parking outside in the huge, paved driveway, she'd seen the black spots car that her partner usually drove when he was called out after hours. He was currently standing near the center of the room, taking pictures of the body. His name was Jake Sullivan, a thirty-one-year-old agent who'd formerly been a P.I. He had a strenuous eye for detail and, so far, was the only agent who had been able to work alongside Tessa without getting irritated or emotionally exhausted. Rather scrawny and socially awkward, he made up for such shortcomings with his candor and attention to small details.

"Hey, Jake."

Jake looked up and nodded. "Always a pleasure. Hey, I hear you killed about nine different records on the obstacle course today."

"News travels fast, I guess."

She'd always appreciated Jake's efforts to have normalized, almost friendly conversations with her even though he knew she struggled with it. Especially when she was at a crime scene. Even now, looking around the room and studying it, any sort of banter with her work partner of nearly a year now was the furthest thing from her mind.

"Flash on that corner, please," she directed Jake. He walked over to the far corner she was pointing at, and the camera shutter clicked obediently in response. Shadows leapt at the command of the flash, revealing subtle incongruities that the untrained eye might miss.

"Local P.D. thinks it's a robbery gone wrong," Jake muttered, but Tessa was already shaking her head. She'd approached the body, which was lying on a velvet chaise. She was quite pretty, though most of it was the work of expensive makeup and plastic surgery. Tessa estimated her to be fifty or so. Her brown hair was colored, the grey just barely showing at the roots.

"Name?" Tessa asked.

"Regina Flowers," Jake said. "Forty-nine years old. A wealthy widow that has sort of fallen out of the eye of the rich spotlight."

Tessa took the information in as she studied and instantly got into the thick of it.

"Look here," Tessa said, voice low but firm as she gestured at the victim's neck. "This wasn't an amateur's frantic grab for valuables." Her latex-clad finger traced the cruel indentation left behind—a perfect replica of the pearls that once adorned Regina's throat. "Strangulation... deliberate, almost ceremonial."

Jake leaned in, squinting. "Could it have been the necklace itself that was used to strangle her?"

"Exactly," Tessa affirmed. The pattern was too precise, the symmetry too intentional. She pictured the killer, painstakingly tightening the strand of pearls, a grim jeweler fastening a final clasp of death. It would have been a very expensive strand, too, not to snap under such pressure. Just like the first victim, Mary Rogers.

With each observation, Tessa felt the tendrils of the killer's psyche winding around her own thoughts. This was no mere thief; this was someone who found artistry in the grotesque, someone who reveled in a twisted exhibition of power and control.

She moved closer, her gaze latching onto the victim's wrists, noting the delicate blue tinge beneath the skin. "And here—do you see? An injection mark," she declared, her mind already racing ahead. "Our killer wanted her immobile but aware. It was pain administered with precision before the final act."

Jake approached, his own eyes following Tessa's pointing finger to the small puncture wound dotting the socialite's pale skin. It was nearly hidden by the glint of her diamond bracelet, but to Tessa, it might as well have been lit by neon signs.

"Jesus," Jake exhaled, his own discomfort palpable in the face of such calculated cruelty.

"He incapacitates them, forces them to be conscious witnesses to their own demise. It's personal, intimate even. He cherishes the pearls—items these women adore—as instruments of their end. A perverse intimacy."

She crouched to examine the victim's neck, where bruises whispered tales of struggle beneath the string of gleaming orbs. "But there's more to it than just control." Her fingers hovered above but never touched, respecting the sanctity of evidence. "These aren't random trinkets; they mean something to him."

"Like a memory?" Jake ventured, leaning in closer to catch every word.

"Or an obsession borne from one," Tessa replied, straightening up. Her silhouette cast long shadows across the polished floor, and for a moment, she seemed as much a part of the crime scene tapestry as the victim herself.

"Perhaps they remind him of someone—mother, lover, someone who wielded power over him once." Her voice had softened, almost empathetic, but her eyes remained sharp, analytical. "And now he's reversing roles, donning the mantle of the oppressor with these very symbols."

"Symbolic retribution," Jake concluded, realization dawning in his tone.

"More than that," Tessa said, stepping back, her hands clasped behind her as she surveyed the scene. "It's a cycle. With each woman, each pearl, he's attempting to rewrite a narrative only he can see."

Tessa felt that familiar surge of adrenaline, the kind that sharpened her senses and set her pulse quickening. It was the rush of the chase, the puzzle beginning to yield its secrets beneath her relentless scrutiny. She allowed herself a moment's satisfaction, knowing that each detail brought her closer to understanding the monster they were hunting. Her thoughts were a whirlwind, piecing together the fragments of a killer's fractured mind. They were dealing with someone who craved not just the act of killing but the theatrics of it, imbuing each murder with a disturbing personal touch.

"Power and pain," she whispered, more to herself than to her partner. "That's what he leaves behind."

As Jake continued documenting the scene, Tessa's eyes lingered on the ghostly outline where the necklace had once lain against flesh, now marred by violence. The killer was out there, weaving a narrative of death and decoration, and Tessa knew that it was her calling to rewrite the ending.

She continued to study the grandeur of the victim's living room, a stark contrast to the dead body in their midst. As Jake meticulously bagged evidence, Tessa's mind raced, drawing lines between the unseen dots. She briefly thought back to the conference room today, where she'd looked over the string of confounding code.

"Jake," she called over her shoulder. "The location, the victims' status... it screams pattern. The killer isn't just choosing wealthy women. I think he's selecting those who are *seen*—people who matter in society."

"Like they're trophies?" Jake suggested, his voice steady despite the gravity of their conversation.

"Exactly," Tessa nodded, her eyes narrowing in thought. "These murders are performances, and the stage is as important as the act. I think that's why he's taking the pearls. Not just to steal them and have them for their value. It's all part of his twisted exhibition."

“Oh, and speaking of trophies…” Jake's voice pulled her from her thoughts as he gestured towards the jewelry box on the vanity. It lay open; its contents spilled out in haste—a chaotic cascade of gemstones and gold. Yet there, amongst the disarray, were several pearl necklaces, similar in size and luster.

"Every victim owned one," Tessa mused aloud. "It's a signature. He leaves one, takes one. Maybe he believes these pearls are his due. A fixation on wealthy women... it's as if he's claiming what he feels was denied to him. The pearls, the pain they're subjected to—it's about power. Control. These women are marionettes in his twisted performance."

Jake nodded, his movements deliberate as he scribbled notes, yet he could not mask the unease in his eyes. Her words painted a psychological portrait too real to ignore.

"Control through pain..." he echoed, underlining the phrase twice.

A heavy silence settled between them, punctuated only by the soft clicks of Jake's camera shutter. Each flash cast a new shadow across the ornate furniture as if exposing the secrets hidden within the room's opulence.

In the midst of this contemplation, Jake's voice cut through once more, "Tess, look at this." He gestured towards the plush carpet where a single pearl glistened against the fibers—a defiant star in a darkening sky.

"Is that—?"

"Part of her necklace, I think," Jake replied. "It must have come loose during the strangulation."

Tessa crouched beside him, a latex-gloved finger delicately rolling the pearl aside. "Or," she said, her voice dropping to a whisper, "it was left for us to find.”

“How so?”

She picked it up and placed it against the indentations on Regina Flowers’ throat. It was noticeably larger than the pearls that had been used to kill her. “This one is different from the rest; see the irregularity? It's deliberate."

"Maybe the killer's calling card?" Jake asked, his brow furrowing as he peered closer.

"Maybe. Or a message. He's arrogant, laying breadcrumbs because he believes he's untouchable. Like I said…it's a performance to him. And what's the point of performing if you don't have an audience?"

"Let's get it to the lab," Jake said, reaching into his over-the-shoulder satchel for an evidence bag.

As Jake secured the pearl, Tessa's thoughts coiled tightly around the enigma of the killer's motive. It wasn't just wealth or beauty that drew him; it was something about these women that reflected his own darkness back at him.

"Did you find anything else of note?" Tessa asked.

"Nothing. Just a few hairs that I'm all but certain are going to end up belonging to the victim. No forced entry, no prints of any kind. Just that damned pearl."

"Then let's wrap up here," she said, her voice echoing with newfound resolve. "He left us that pearl on purpose. So if he wants to play a game with us, let's play. I'll run this to the lab. Are you okay to get more details on the house?"

"Sure thing," he said, already bringing the camera up to his eye to snap another picture.

As Jake snapped a few more photos of the crime scene, Tessa's mind churned with theories and questions. The room spoke of elegance and horror in equal measure, but to Tessa, it was now a roadmap—one that led into the darkest recesses of a killer's mind. She glanced once more at Regina Flowers, and made a silent vow to unravel this puzzle before another life could be taken.

CHAPTER THREE

As she exited the house, the night air clung to her skin, a shroud of impending dread. The drive to the FBI lab was a blur, her thoughts racing faster than the engine's hum. Tessa replayed every detail, every whispered word between her and Jake, searching for the slip—the crack in the killer's meticulous armor.

And with the night and highway speeding along behind her, she again found her memories slipping back to her childhood. Her crying parents, the befuddled doctors. It had all started with Tessa running through the field behind her grandmother's house, her right leg falling into a hole in the ground where yellow jackets had made a nest. She'd been stung sixteen times, and though the doctors had dosed her up with medicine in the event of allergies, Tessa never felt a thing. Not the stings and bites from the yellow jackets, not the twist of her ankle in the hole, not the injection of medicine at the doctor's office.

Despite countless doctor's visits and trips to specialists all over the country, a fitting diagnosis had never been found. The closest and most fitting diagnosis was Congenital insensitivity to pain and anhidrosis—or CIPA. However, her condition went beyond such a diagnosis. Patients diagnosed with CIPA—which was an incredibly rare condition—typically suffered from fevers and infections. A small percentage also suffered from mental abnormalities and challenges. But not Tessa. She'd always been the portrait of perfect health.

As she grew older, many specialists implored her to take part in studies, claiming she was a medical marvel. Someone who could not feel pain but was also not presenting the illnesses and obstacles that others with CIPA experienced. It had been discovered that, like CIPA patients, the pain-sensing nerves in her brain weren't wired properly. But without the ailments that typically came with it, she was quite different.

It meant that when she broke her arm in tenth grade, all she'd felt was a strange tingling sensation in the initial fifteen minutes upon breaking the bone. It meant she didn't feel the effect of punches she doled out, or the way the ropes of the obstacle course burned at her hand when she raced up them to obliterate records set before her.

And it also meant that, without the worry of pain, she was far more willing to throw herself into dangerous cases—to hunt down maniacal killers like this one.

The flow of her memories swept her to the bureau lab. The building was a sprawling fortress of science, including the mineralogy division, where secrets etched in stone and sediment were coaxed into confession. Tessa navigated through a labyrinth of sterile corridors with the bagged pearl in her pocket. She could almost feel it pulsating as if it harbored the essence of its previous owner—a silent witness begging to be heard.

Upon reaching the mineralogy division, the air bore a different kind of weight, laden with the scent of metal and Earth. Fluorescent lights buzzed overhead, casting a clinical glow on rows of high-powered microscopes and spectrometers.

"Dr. Carter?" she called out, finding the forensics expert hunched over a geological map speckled with color-coded pins.

Lucas Carter glanced up, his eyes the shade of smoky quartz, reflecting a life spent peering into the very soul of the Earth. "Agent Flint," he greeted, pushing back his chair with a scrape that echoed off the walls. "I got a call that you were on the way. I understand you've got something interesting for me."

"Maybe." Tessa placed the pearl into Dr. Carter's outstretched hand. "I need to know everything about this pearl. Its origin could be pivotal to our case."

Lucas held it up to the light, squinting as he rotated it between his fingers. "Hmm, not your run-of-the-mill gemstone," he said thoughtfully. "But…hmm. Well, this might take some time."

He moved towards a microscope, beckoning Tessa to follow. She watched as Dr. Carter placed the pearl onto the slide and peered through the eyepiece. His brows furrowed, a testament to the puzzle before him. After he had a look, he nodded over to a small laptop situated a few feet away from the microscope, sitting near the edge of the workstation. It showed what Lucas was looking at through the microscope.

"See here?" Lucas adjusted the focus and pointed to the screen displaying the magnified image of the pearl's surface. "The concentric layering is too perfect. Nature's handiwork is rarely this meticulous."

"Are we looking at a cultured pearl then?" Tessa leaned in closer, her reflection mingling with the magnified image on the screen.

"Potentially," Lucas replied. "But the environment in which it was cultivated, the specific methods used... those details can give us more context." He tapped the side of the microscope pensively. "We'll need to run some tests—check for trace elements, maybe even DNA."

"Whatever it takes," Tessa affirmed, her resolve hardening. She trusted Lucas's expertise as much as she trusted her own instincts. If this pearl was indeed a message from the killer, the science would help her decode it.

"Let's get started then." Lucas eyed her with a mix of respect and shared determination.

Tessa stepped to the side, leaving Lucas to his work. There wasn't exactly a waiting room in the mineralogy department, but there was a central space among it all, a hub of sterile surfaces and scientific rigor. Tessa allowed herself a moment—just one—to breathe. But rest was a luxury she couldn't afford, not with a killer's clock ticking somewhere in the shadows. And the recent onslaught of memories from her past wasn't helping either. Sure, so far, it had all dealt with her condition—her inability to feel pain—but she worried that thoughts of her sister wouldn't be far behind.

And if she allowed herself to delve into thoughts of her sister or, more specifically, her sister's disappearance, she knew she'd completely lose focus on this case. Her sister was a dark seed that she kept pushed down when she could because when she brought it to light, it consumed her. And she'd been able to avoid that for years now.

Still…her sister…the questions surrounding her. How was she supposed to simply let it go? How could she—

"Quite the waiting game, huh?" Dr. Lucas Carter's voice broke through her contemplation as he stepped beside her, handing her a cup of coffee that smelled like a lifeline.

"Thanks," she murmured, cradling the warmth. "Waiting is part of the job, but it doesn't get easier."

"Especially with what's at stake." Lucas leaned against a counter, sipping his coffee with calculated casualness. "I've got a program running a few things right now. Seems like I'll be waiting a bit, too."

At the same moment, her cell phone rang. She checked the caller display and saw that it was Jake. "Excuse me a moment," she said, stepping away with her cup of coffee. She stood in the corner of the room and took the call. "Hey, Jake."

"Hey. So I'm leaving Regina Flowers' residence. I think I'm going to head to the office and start comparing notes and crime scene photos from this scene and the Mary Rogers scene. Are you still at the lab?"

“I am. And you know…Jake, both of our victims were from high-end gated communities, exclusive... almost fortresses designed to keep danger out. And yet..."

"Yet the killer walked right in," Jake finished for her. "You think that's part of his message?"

"Maybe. Or maybe it's about who they were—wealthy, protected, untouchable until he touched them."

"Patterns are killers' signatures," Jake pointed out. "And this one's signing in bold."

"Exactly." Tessa set her coffee down, untouched, and began to pace the room, her boots clicking methodically on the tile floor, echoing the cadence of her thoughts. "Victim one, Mary Rogers, A successful businesswoman in her forties who was admired in her community for her philanthropy. Victim two, Regina Flowers, a wealthy socialite who fell out of favor with the upper-class community. Both pillars of their communities at one point. Both are high-ranking in their circles. And both... targets."

"Because of their wealth, you think?” Jake asked. “Could it be that simple?”

"Perhaps," Tessa mused, stopping to glance at the monitors displaying the magnified image of the pearl. "Wealth might be the thread—it ties them together, makes them stand out. So maybe the killer is making a statement by infiltrating these bastions of safety and privilege. He's challenging their status. But why?"

"Envy? Revenge?"

"Could be," she conceded. "But we'll need more than speculation. We need to dig deeper into their lives, find the connection beyond their bank accounts."

“And that’s what I’ll be doing at the office. You coming by when you’re done at the lab?”

“Maybe. I’ll keep you posted.” She noticed that Lucas had gone back to his station, moving on to the next step in the process. “Bye for now, Jake.”

She ended the call, hoping Lucas might have answers, but he had simply moved the pearl to another machine, another station. She walked over to the work area and pointed to one of several laptops not currently in use.

“Lucas, do you mind if I use one to get on the bureau’s mobile server?”

“Help yourself. I’m getting close to being one here, but I hesitate to give you an estimate.”

Tessa sat down at the laptop and pulled up the dedicated server the bureau allowed their agents to use while out in the field. The fluorescent lights of the FBI lab buzzed overhead, a deadpan chorus ushering her toward the police reports for Mary Rogers' murder. She found them easy enough, as they were recent and active. She scrolled through the local police reports, looking for anything that stood out..

The cogs in her mind whirred as she dissected every element of the initial investigation at the home of Mary Rogers. The first detective had been thorough, but his notes hinted at a haste shaped by the pressure of the affluent community's watchful eyes. Tessa could feel it—the itch of something just beyond reach, the whisper of silk sliding across a jagged edge. His notes were thorough and precise. She noted that the first officer on the scene mentioned a painting, a Monet, was askew. Everyone assumed it happened during the struggle, but because of the pearl that had been left behind for them at Regina Flowers' home, Tessa wondered if the crooked painting might have been intentional. Maybe a message of some kind.

Her mind spun a web of possibilities, each more sinister than the last. Wealth, art, precision—all pieces of a puzzle only she could assemble. With each theory, Tessa wove a clearer picture of the shadow they chased, a specter dancing just out of sight, cloaked in the trappings of high society.

She wasn't sure how long she' been looking through the files wen Lucas finally came back, but she knew at least three hours had passed since she came through the doors of the lab.

"Got something for you, Flint," Dr. Carter announced, striding toward her borrowed workstation with a sheaf of printouts that crackled in his grip.

"Tell me it's good news," Tessa said, though her tone betrayed her expectation of anything but.

"Depends on your definition of 'good.' It's not natural," he replied, setting the papers down before her with deliberate care. "This pearl... it's a cultured creation. Exceptionally rare, grown with a technique known only to a few high-caliber jewelers."

The words hung heavy between them, laden with implications that stretched far beyond the confines of the lab. Tessa's mind raced, piecing together the fragments of information.

"Can we trace it?" Her voice was steady, belying the storm of thoughts within.

"Maybe. But it's not going to be easy. This kind of craftsmanship... it's signature work. Exclusive clientele," Dr. Carter explained, his own eyes narrowing as he considered the magnitude of their discovery.

Tessa leaned forward, her eyes scanning the detailed analysis of the pearl's structure, the unique signature of its creation etched into its very core.

"Exclusive," she echoed softly, her pulse quickening. “So maybe a jeweler?”

“As the killer?” Lucas asked.

"Maybe. And if not, at the very least, a valuable source of information as to who would buy such a string of pearls. Or who would *kill* for them.”

She looked back to the screen, looking at the pearl, although Lucas had laid it back down, protected in the evidence bag once again, with the papers. The pearl was a vital clue, a breadcrumb left behind by a murderer who cloaked his savagery in luxury. And now, it pointed them towards a man who crafted beauty with his hands yet may well wield death just as skillfully.

CHAPTER FOUR

Tessa sat hunched over her laptop, her fingers flying across the keys with a focus that had become almost second nature. The glow of the screen set her sharp features in stark relief against the darkened backdrop of the precinct's records room. Jake was sifting through physical files, his brow furrowed in concentration.

"Found anything yet?" Tessa asked without looking up, her voice betraying a hint of impatience.

"Nothing solid," Jake replied, flipping another page. "Just names and shop numbers."

"Same here. And the only illegal activity I'm coming across is break-ins and thefts. Nothing shady about the owners or dealers."

"Then we just keep digging," Jake said. "It's such a niche thing to be looking for that we're bound to come up with something."

And that's exactly what they did, searching for anyone within a fifty-mile radius that had both a criminal history or any sort of connection with jewelers or jewelry stores. They'd agreed from the start that their last case scenario would be to simply go door-to-door to all jewelry stores in the area tomorrow morning, but that would take up a lot of time. If they could narrow the list down substantially, they'd save a lot of time—and maybe a life or two.

"Ah, bingo," Jake said, slapping at a file folder in triumph. "Vincent Crabtree. He has a boutique just outside of the city…known specifically for unique and hard-to-find pieces. And four years ago, he was arrested for assault and battery on his very young girlfriend."

Tessa knew it wasn't an incredibly strong lead, but it was the best they'd had yet. She pulled up Crabtree's website, eyeing the jewels displayed with an aesthetic that whispered of wealth and secrets. Lo and behold, there were numerous pictures of gorgeous pearls.

"His clientele list is private," Tessa said. "But if he's our guy, I bet he won't be able to resist showing off his work."

"Let's pay Mr. Crabtree a visit first thing tomorrow," Jake said, a strategic glint in her eye.

"Agreed," Tessa nodded. "I'll arrange everything."

As the night deepened around them, Tessa couldn't shake off the ominous feeling creeping up her spine. The hunt was on, and the stakes were higher than ever. With each unsolved murder weighing heavily on her conscience, she knew there was no room for errors. This jeweler, Vincent Crabtree, could be the break they needed—or another dead end that would set them right back to the start.

***

The morning sun cast a golden sheen over the bustling city streets as Tessa approached the grand facade of Crabtree's Fine Jewelry. She paused momentarily, allowing herself to be just another face in the crowd, her sharp gaze absorbing every detail of the high-end boutique that stood before her like a fortress of opulence.

"Looks like he caters to the elite," Jake murmured, sidling up beside her with a faux casualness that didn't quite reach his alert eyes.

"Let's see if his pearls are as exclusive as his clientele," Tessa replied, her tone light but her mind racing with the gravity of their task.

Together, they stepped through the threshold of the shop, the door chiming a welcome. The interior was a testament to luxury—a gleaming palace of glass and marble, where the softest lighting caressed each display case like a lover's touch. Precious stones sparkled from their velvet-lined homes, beckoning with silent promises of wealth and beauty.

"Can I help you?" a smooth voice cut through the hushed reverence of the showroom.

"Mr. Crabtree, I presume?" Tessa asked, turning towards the source of the voice.

The man who approached them was middle-aged, dressed impeccably in a tailored suit that spoke of custom fittings and expensive tastes. His smile was practiced, but his eyes held a calculating sheen that immediately set Tessa on edge. This was their suspect, the jeweler who might hold the key to unlocking the string of brutal murders that had left the city on edge. It didn't bode well that she felt uneasy about him at first sight.

"That's me," he said. "What can I do for you today?"

"I'm interested in pearls," Tessa said, letting the lie roll off her tongue with practiced ease. "My fiancé here has exceptional taste."

Jake slipped his arm around her waist, playing his part with convincing affection. It wasn't the first time they'd played parts undercover like this before, so there was a comfortable ease to the act. "The best for my future bride," Jake added with a charismatic grin.

Tessa found herself having to bite back a grin.

"Ah, pearls it is then," Crabtree said, leading them over to a section of the store that seemed to shimmer with an inner light. "A timeless choice. Pearls symbolize purity, elegance... and mystery."

His fingers lingered over a strand of perfectly round pearls, the admiration in his gaze bordering on obsessive. It was more than the look of a craftsman appreciating his work; there was an intensity to his fixation that seemed almost... personal.

"Beautiful," Tessa breathed, feigning wonder as she leaned closer to inspect the jewelry. "Where do you find such exquisite pieces?"

"Only the finest suppliers," Crabtree replied, his voice dropping to a conspiratorial whisper. "The rarity of these gems can't be understated. Like snowflakes, no two are the same."

"Is that so?" Jake chimed in. "They say every beautiful thing has its secrets."

"Indeed," Crabtree agreed. His eyes darkened for a moment before he recovered his composure. "But let's focus on finding something perfect for your lovely companion, shall we?"

As they continued to peruse the selection, Tessa's mind whirred. There was something about the man's demeanor—his fervent adoration of the pearls—that resonated with an eerie familiarity. She couldn't shake the feeling that beneath the polished surface of this jeweler lurked shadows that went far deeper than mere aesthetic appreciation.

"Tell us, Mr. Crabtree," Tessa ventured, watching him closely. "Do you keep records of your clients? Anyone who might share our passion for these beauties?"

"Confidentiality is paramount in this business," Crabtree replied, his lips curving into a tight smile. "Rest assured, our clientele value their privacy."

"Of course," Jake agreed smoothly. "Discretion is everything."

Tessa nodded, but inside, her doubt grew. Despite the unsettling vibe Crabtree exuded, she couldn't ignore the niggling sensation at the back of her mind that warned her not to rush to judgment. Her gut told her that the killer they sought was meticulous, cunning—a predator who thrived on control. Crabtree's odd behavior could simply be the eccentricity of an artist lost in his craft. But was it possible that they were looking at the wrong man?

She needed to push further to find the crack in the facade—if there was one. The answer lay hidden somewhere among the glittering displays and Crabtree's cryptic words. Tessa's gaze flicked over the gleaming glass cases, each one a treasure trove of potential leads, before settling back on Crabtree. She could sense Jake tensing beside her, ready for whatever might come next.

"Mr. Crabtree," Jake said, his voice steady but with an edge that suggested he wasn't just here to admire the merchandise. "I'm sure you understand our concern. Pearls like these," he gestured towards a necklace that shimmered with an inner light, "they're not common."

Crabtree's eyes narrowed, a muscle twitching in his jaw. He leaned in, his breath carrying the faint scent of polishing compound. "And what, exactly, is your concern?"

"Your pearls are beautiful," Tessa interjected, hoping to defuse the building tension. "But we've seen similar ones recently... under less-than-ideal circumstances."

A shadow crossed Crabtree's face, and without warning, he lunged at Jake, his hands clawing for something concealed beneath his apron. Despite the absolute shock of the moment, Jake reacted instinctively, grabbing the jeweler's wrists and twisting. The two men grappled, bodies slamming against the glass counters with a dreadful sound that threatened to shatter more than just the opulent facade of the boutique.

What the hell? Tessa wondered. What had possibly set Crabtree off? Had he assumed they were accusing him of selling stolen or counterfire merchandise? She didn't know. All she knew for sure was that he had snapped *fast.* The man was impatient and had a violent streak in him, without a doubt.

"Stop this!" Tessa shouted, moving closer. Her heart pounded, but she didn't hesitate. She couldn't let this spiral any further out of control—not when they were so close to finding answers.

As Jake and Crabtree struggled by one of the display cases, Tessa saw her chance and reached for Crabtree's flailing arm, trying to pry him off Jake. But the motion was too forceful, too desperate, and she stumbled. She caught herself by the forearm on the glass case. The glass shattered, and her arm went through, the glass tearing through the long sleeve of her shirt and ripping at her flesh.

For a moment, everything stopped. Tessa pulled herself free from the wreckage, shards of glass clinging to her clothes like icy droplets. She should have been in agony, cuts webbing across her arm from elbow to wrist and blood welling up—but there was nothing. No pain. Only the sharp clarity of adrenaline and the realization that both men were now staring at her.

"Are you alright?" Jake gasped, finally subduing Crabtree with a firm grip and a twist of the jeweler's arm behind his back. Crabtree let out a weak cry as Jake arched his back and forced him to stand straight up with the arm pulled tight behind him.

Tessa rose, brushing off slivers of glass. "I'm fine," she said, more to reassure herself than Jake. She did, however, wait until he wasn't looking directly at her to dislodge a rather large shard from her flesh. Her condition had always been her secret armor—and now it lay exposed amidst the remnants of Crabtree's precious collection. Jake, of course, had known about ever since they' started working together but he never seemed to get used to it.

Currently, her arm was dripping blood, her shirt soaking it in. Idly, she wondered if she'd need stitches. More than that, though, she also reminded herself that despite the lack of pain, this was something she needed to take seriously. One wound gone untreated could lead to a nasty infection, and nasty infections could often get very complicated. She'd had enough of those particular situations in her youth. There was a particular moment when she'd stepped on the edge of a rusted tin can without knowing it and had spent two days in the hospital fighting a fever and infection.

As Crabtree cursed and railed against Jake's hold, Tessa surveyed the damage. Her intervention may have seemed reckless, but it was done. And while Crabtree might have been suspect number one, Tessa's instincts still whispered that there was more to the story than a violent jeweler with a penchant for pearls.

As Jake cuffed Crabtree out among the glittering glass cases, Tessa stepped over the threshold into Crabtree's office. It was located down a shallow corridor behind the last of the cases. The room was an antiquated sanctuary choked with the smell of leather and varnish, a far cry from the polished glass and gleam outside. All around her, the walls were lined with oiled wood panels, their grain running like dark rivers beneath the weight of framed accolades and faded photographs of Crabtree shaking hands with the city's elite.

"This is an absolute outrage," Crabtree began, his voice muffled as Jake guided him toward the office. "You have no right—"

"Quiet," Tessa snapped without looking back, her focus narrowing on the task at hand.

She moved with precision, her gaze flitting across the expanse of the heavy desk dominating the center of the room, skimming over invoices, letters, and scribbled notes. Her fingers danced deftly through drawers, rifling for anything out of place, anything that could tie

Crabtree to the meticulously staged murder scenes, but nothing screamed 'guilty.'

"Find anything?" Jake grunted, struggling to keep Crabtree still.

"Still searching," she replied, her voice steady despite the storm of doubt beginning to brew within her. Instinctually, she'd pulled the sleeve of her right arm tight against her skin, creating a very shoddy tourniquet of sorts. She found herself willing something sinister to surface, some shred of evidence to vindicate the violence, the shattered glass, the blood now drying on her skin.

Her eyes caught a glimpse of the safe tucked behind a painting, its edges protruding just so. But when she swung the frame aside, the safe was locked, its combination dial staring back at her mockingly. There was no time to crack it now, and she didn't see Crabtree just coming up with the combination for them.

"Nothing conclusive," Tessa reported, a twinge of frustration lacing her words. "We need a warrant to open that safe."

"Then we'll get one," Jake assured her, pulling Crabtree up by his cuffed wrists.

As Crabtree began another tirade, claiming mistreatment, Tessa tuned him out and retreated into the quiet space of her mind where profiles and patterns lived. She had constructed a psychological maze for the killer, one that Crabtree didn't seem to navigate with the ease she had anticipated. His fixation with pearls was certainly odd, yet his ego and pride in his work did not align with the cold calculation of the crimes. And his violent outburst wasn't helping him, either.

"You two better damn well tell me what this is all about! Are you cops? Detectives?"

"FBI agents," Tessa said. "And we're investigating two murders that seem to have pearl necklaces at their center."

"What? And you think I have something to do with it?"

"Well, your hot-headed actions out front aren't helping matters," Jake said.

"any chance you want to tell us what's in that safe?"

"Money and personal papers."

"That's all?" Tessa asked.

"Yes!"

"Then give me the combination."

Crabtree fought one last time against Jake, to no avail. "Go to hell," he said.

Tessa sighed and looked back to the safe once more. The truth was locked away, either inside that metal box or somewhere in the depths of a killer's twisted mind. And she would uncover it, one way or another.

CHAPTER FIVE

The scent of freshly cut grass hung in the air as Tessa stepped out of the unmarked bureau sedan. A mower buzzed nearby as a lawn maintenance company served a client in the cool of the summer morning. Her gaze swept over the elegant facade of the Flowers' residence. It looked quite different in the daylight, but she doubted the feeling of the interior would have changed much since last night.

She and Jake had assumed the best thing to do while waiting for the warrant to check Crabtree's safe would be to question Regina Flowers' husband. Jake had received a call earlier, letting him know that the husband—who'd been flying into the city from a business trip when she was killed—was home and ready to speak.

They walked up the sidewalk together, both knowing how emotionally exhausting it could be to speak to the loved ones of those who had just been murdered.

"Are you okay to do this?" Jake asked.

"Of course. Why wouldn't I be?"

He pointed to her bandaged arm. She'd used the strips of gauze and medical tape from the first aid kit in the trunk of their car. A bit of blood had seeped through, but that was about it. She didn't think the cuts would require stitches, and because the pain the cuts *should* have caused was non-existent to her, she really didn't see the so-called injury as a big deal. But while her pain receptors might be defective, but the adrenaline pumping through her veins was very much alive.

"Yes, it's fine."

He nodded, choosing to say nothing. He knew about her odd condition and thought he'd asked simple questions in the past, and he'd never been invasive about it. It was one of the many reasons Tessa respected him as much as she did. He knew when to pry and when to keep quiet.

When they reached the front door, painted a dark brown with a gold knocker in its center, Jake knocked. The door was answered right away, swinging open to reveal the grief-stricken husband. Wayne Flowers was slightly older than his deceased wife. He was clean-shaven, and his greying hair was a bit of a mess. He looked tired, and his eyes were bloodshot.

"You're the agents?" Wayne Flowers asked.

"Yes," Tessa said. "Agents Flint and Sullivan. Can we come in?"

Wayne said nothing but waved them inside. As he led them into the living room, Tessa took note of the fine art adorning the walls, the plush furniture, and the glint of high-end decor—it was like stepping into a page from a luxury magazine, all too familiar. She had, of course, noted it all before, but she thought it more necessary than ever to take note of these things, especially if something as grandiose as expensive pearls were at the center of this case.

Regina's body had, of course, been moved since she and Jake had been in this same room last night. She also noted that Wayne had chosen to remove the chair on which his wife' dead body had been splayed.

"Mr. Flowers, we're deeply sorry for your loss," Tessa began, infusing her voice with as much warmth as she could muster. "We hope to catch whoever did this to your wife, and speaking to you is going to go a long way to achieving that."

"Thank you, detectives," Wayne said, his voice brittle as thin ice. "I... I still can't believe she's gone. I'd been gone for three days—in New York on business—and when I landed at eight this morning, my phone was filled with voicemails. From the cops, from family, from…" He sighed shakily, fighting off tears, and finished: "I just can't believe it."

"We understand this is difficult," Jake chimed in, "but anything you can tell us about her would help. Her habits, her friends, grudges against others…anything like that might help us find answers."

Wayne sighed, running a hand through his hair. "Regina lived for the finer things—parties, jewelry, fashion. She loved to be seen and envied." His gaze drifted, lost in the painful memories. "I know that doesn't paint her in the best light, but I figure brutal honesty is what you're after, right?"

"It is," Tessa said.

"I suppose you know that she had something of a fall from grace. Rumors about her sleeping around and ruining marriages. People started seeing her in a bad light, and she'd become a shut-in."

"Was there any truth to the rumors?" Jake asked.

"None that I ever found. And I did spend a good deal of time looking."

"Did she share this love for extravagance with anyone in particular? Someone who might have envied her a bit too much?" Tessa asked, watching the widower closely.

"Everyone admired her," he responded with a hollow laugh. "I think it's why the rumors all started…out of jealousy, you know? But Regina didn't have enemies outside of whoever started those rumors. She just... shined too brightly."

As the conversation ebbed and flowed around Regina Flowers' social whirlwind, Tessa's mind sorted through the implications. Wealth had been a glowing beacon for the killer, drawing him like a moth to a flame. It was more than a coincidence; it was a pattern. The question remained, though…was he drawn to it out of envy or hatred?

"Thank you, Mr. Flowers," Tessa said, her voice steady despite the turmoil in her thoughts. "We'll do everything to bring justice for Regina. For now, though, I wonder if Agent Sullivan and I could have a look around. Maybe see the bedroom?"

"Sure."

"Did she perhaps have a study or office?"

"She did," Wayne said. "This way."

He led them out of the living room and down a grand hallway. They were flanked by extravagant paintings and sculptures that seemed to mock the solemnity of the situation with their silent, gilded beauty. Under Wayne's watchful gaze, they entered a home office. It was carpeted and beautiful curtains hung from a window that looked out onto the side yard and a flowerbed.

As she started to look around, Tessa noticed that Wayne would not come in. He stood at the doorway, looking in and grieving. Tessa looked to the beautifully arrange desk, a laptop and large planner in the center. Beside it was a gorgeous mahogany drawer. Tessa's fingers grazed the cool, smooth wood as she searched for anything that might whisper a clue.

"Is it necessary to go through her personal items?" Wayne asked. His voice was tinged with a mix of grief and indignation, echoing in the spacious room adorned with lush fabrics and polished surfaces.

"Every detail could be crucial," Tessa replied, not lifting her eyes from the task at hand. "I assure you we handle these matters with utmost respect."

Her hand brushed against something unexpected in the drawer—a soft, hidden compartment at the back. With deliberate care, she tugged it free, revealing a velvet pouch that cradled its contents like a secret.

As she unfolded the plush material, a strand of pearls cascaded into her palm, their luster dimmed by the shadow of death that clung to them.

"Weird..." Jake muttered, his voice low, mirroring Tessa's thoughts.

"Detective Flint?" Wayne leaned forward, curiosity momentarily overriding his sorrow.

"Similar to what we found at the crime scene," Tessa explained, holding the necklace up to the light. The pearls told a story of wealth—and perhaps, a motive, given that they'd been hidden.

"May I?" Wayne reached out, a tremor in his hand betraying his composure.

Tessa obliged, watching his reaction closely as he touched the necklace, his eyes clouding with unspoken memories.

It was a coincidence, sure. Another pearl necklace, another wealthy victim. But surely most women with lots of money would likely have pearl necklaces, right?

"Could this have been what the killer intended to use?" she murmured, more to herself than to the men in the room.

"Intended to use?" Wayne echoed.

"Tell me…would it have been a common thing for Regina to wear a pearl necklace around the house?"

Wayne thought about it for a moment and shrugged. "I…I don't think so. It depends on whether or not she'd gone out that night. And, as I said, she hadn't done much going out as of late."

Tessa considered this seriously for the first time. What if she hadn't been *wearing* a necklace when she was killed? What if the killer had brought his own necklace and used it as a weapon to strangle her?

Tessa's investigator instinct kicked into high gear. If the killer had indeed gained entry into the homes before committing the murders, it meant they were likely someone trusted, someone who wouldn't raise suspicion. That revelation sent a ripple of alarm through her because it wasn't just about finding a murderer anymore—it was about unveiling a predator hiding in plain sight among the glittering facades of wealth.

"Mr. Flowers," Tessa said, her tone steady despite the racing of her heart, "can you think of anyone who would have had access to such personal belongings? Staff, friends, even family?"

Wayne shook his head, the lines of his face deepening with distress. "No one I can think of. We trusted our staff and our friends... they had no reason."

"Sometimes the reasons aren't as clear-cut as we'd like them to be," Tessa offered gently, her thoughts churning. The killer was meticulous, cunning—the kind of person who could orchestrate a facade as convincing as the smiles in the portraits that lined the walls of this house.

A shiver ran down her spine, a silent acknowledgment of the hunt that lay ahead. Whoever they were dealing with was a master of deception, a ghost within the machine of high society. And Tessa Flint was determined to drag them into the light.

"Hey, look at this," Jake said from the other side of the room. He was standing by a small yet elegant bookshelf.

He was holding a leatherbound book, the cover opened to the first page. “Looks like a journal,” he said, thumbing through the pages.

“Christ,” Wayne said. “I didn’t even know she kept a journal.”

Tessa walked over to Jake and looked on as he sifted through the pages. The elegant, looping script told countless stories. Together, they scanned pages filled with confessions and fears, a silent testament to a life abruptly severed. Her eyes caught on a passage dated just weeks prior to the murder.

“Go to the back,” Tessa said. “To the most recent.”

He did, and they saw that the final entry was rather boring and not important. In it, Regina was complaining about local politics and not being invited to a particular gala event. However, the entry before that one, dated just eight days ago, caught her eyes.

“That one,” she said, pointing.

Jake nodded, looking at Wayne. Wayne nodded as if urging him to go ahead and read it. Jake cleared his voice and read: "'There's a man—a worker in our community. I don't know his name, but there's something off about him. He watches too closely, lingers where he shouldn't. It's unsettling. I think he’s a gardener for one of the other families, but I don’t know who. Just another example of they’ll let *anyone* work in this awful neighborhood these days. Stupid neighbors.'"

"Creepy worker?" Tessa asked, leaning in. "No name?"

"None. And no clear accusation, just a feeling."

Tessa looked to Wayne, curious. “Did Regina ever mention such a man in the neighborhood to you before?”

He shook his head with a profoundly sad look on his face. “No. And honestly, even if she did, I don’t know that I would have been listening.” With tears rolling down his cheeks, he admitted, “I’ve never been an attentive husband. And now…now it’s too damned late.”

Tessa watched as Jake closed the diary, the leather creaking softly in protest. She knew better than to dismiss gut feelings—especially those penned down with such palpable unease. For that particular entry to be one of her last…surely, it meant something.

"What do you think?" Jake asked.

“I think both women were wealthy, had a taste for luxury, and lived in neighborhoods where almost every lawn is mown by a service. And now we have a victim specifically calling out one such man.”

"Could be a coincidence," Jake countered, though the skepticism didn't quite reach his eyes.

"Or it could be our link," Tessa replied, her gaze hardening. "This 'creepy worker' must have access, familiarity to *at least* this neighborhood. The kind that allows someone to move unnoticed among people who are trained not to see them."

"Staff, gardeners, delivery guys..." Jake listed off potential roles, each one a cog in the machine of the affluent lifestyle.

“And think of Mary Rogers. She was preparing for that party. She had employees and workers going in and out. The police are still interviewing all of them. But clearly, the killer isn’t part of that group because he’s killed again while those workers are being watched and questioned.”

“So…what do we do? Get a list of lawn companies that serve both neighborhoods?”

"Lawn companies, garbage pick-up, internet providers…any company that has workers who have come to both of our victims' homes in the past month or so."

"Alright," Jake nodded, his own resolve mirrored in his partner's determination. "Let's pull the threads then. See what unravels."

Tessa glanced back at the diary, the weight of the deceased's words pressing upon her. Someone out there was taking lives, slipping through the cracks in a world built on appearances. Tessa felt the stirrings of the chase tightening around her heart. She now felt that they were gaining traction but reminded herself that the killer had a huge head start…while she and Jake still had a lot of ground to cover.

CHAPTER SIX

He stood concealed behind the foliage that bordered the well-maintained streets, his gaze sweeping over the pristine expanse of the gated community. From this hidden vantage point, he could watch them—those fortunate souls who lived out their days in careless splendor, ensconced in their palatial homes, buffered from the world's uglier and inconvenient sides by high walls and higher bank balances.

"Perfect, aren't they?" he murmured to himself. A sneer curled his lips as his eyes followed a laughing couple sauntering down the sidewalk. Their designer dog leaped between them, stopping to piss on a mailbox pole.

He shifted his focus, noting with a sense of loathing how the sunlight played off the meticulously maintained lawns, casting emerald glints that seemed to mock him. It was all so artificial, so contrived. Each blade of grass was a testament to the residents' mastery over the world—a domain that *he* had been denied entry into, time and again.

"Work for it," they said. "Earn it." But what did they know of work? Of the grind and sweat it took just to claw one's way up to the precipice of mediocrity, only to be pushed back down? No, they simply existed—floating through life on clouds of unearned privilege.

As he watched, his attention was drawn to a solitary figure tending to a vibrant patch of garden. The retired schoolteacher, Mrs. Edith Harper, with her gray hair tied back and her hands lovingly coaxing life from the soil. She was kneeling beside a bed of roses, her fingers deftly snipping away at the undergrowth.

"Morning, Mrs. Harper!" a voice called out, belonging to one of the passing residents. This one wasn't walking a dog but was wearing one of those ridiculous exercise trackers on her wrist. "Your garden is looking beautiful!"

"Thank you, dear!" she replied, her voice airy and sweet. "Just giving them a little love."

He felt a twinge of something—a pull towards this woman who created beauty with such ease. Her garden was a splash of wildness amidst the order, a piece of Eden carved out of the sterile perfection.

He imagined her hands, gnarled with age and wisdom, working the Earth, imparting bits of her soul into each bloom. There was an artistry there, a quiet dignity that set her apart from the rest of her pampered neighbors.

Delicate and strong, he thought, a plan beginning to form in the recesses of his mind. *Much like those pearls she favors.*

He could see the allure in cultivating such a garden, in nurturing something real amidst the façade. And yet, it was the very realness of it—the fact that it was a labor of love—that made it, and its caretaker, stand out to him. Here, in this place where everything was served on a silver platter, Mrs. Harper chose to get her hands dirty.

And with that thought, he began to deftly move out of the decorative tangle of trees, shrubs, and foliage. He moved to the right, where he knew he would be unseen by anyone when he stepped out behind the gated community's welcome sign. When he stepped onto the sidewalk, his eyes never left Mrs. Harper or her roses.

He was wearing the navy coveralls that bore the logo of the gated community's maintenance team—a serpent coiled around a tree, an ironic nod to some paradise lost. The sun was high and unforgiving, yet he felt only the chill of his intent as he pushed the wheelbarrow filled with gardening tools along the sidewalk. Mrs. Harper's house was just three houses down from the secondary entrance to the community he'd been spying behind.

"Morning," he called out, his voice cheerful but nondescript, the perfect camouflage of amiability. "Beautiful day for some roses, isn't it?"

Mrs. Harper looked up, her expression one of mild curiosity framed by a halo of silver hair. "Oh, I didn't recognize you. Are you new here?" She wiped her brow with a dirt-stained glove.

"First week on the job," he lied smoothly, leaning on the handles of the wheelbarrow. "I couldn't help but notice these—are they Eden Climbers?" He gestured towards the trellis, where blooms of pale pink spilled over like nature's own masterpiece.

"Yes, that's right." Pride twinkled in her eyes. "They need constant care, but the results are well worth it."

He shifted his gaze to her ears, where twin pearls hung—lustrous and iridescent, whispering tales of the sea. His breath caught slightly, the sight of them awakening a familiar hunger. Pearls, the embodiment of elegance and purity, had long since become his grotesque obsession, each one a memento of control and power over lives far removed from his own sordid existence.

"Those earrings are stunning," he complimented, his voice carrying a hint of reverence. "They suit you."

"Thank you," Mrs. Harper responded, blushing at the unexpected flattery. "A gift from my late husband. He always said pearls reflected my spirit." With a smile, she added: "Are you fond of pearls?"

"Very," he answered, his smile now predatory. "Each one tells a story, don't you think? A narrative waiting to be... unearthed."

"Perhaps," she chuckled, turning back to her roses.

As he pretended to inspect the nearby shrubbery, his fingers itched to reach for his collection, to feel the smoothness of his gathered pearls—one for each life taken, soon to be joined by another.

As he pretended to work (he *did* do some work from time to time, but keeping an eye on the wealthy residents was his main goal), the sun dipped lower, casting a golden hue over the polished facades of the houses. But his eyes remained clouded with envy. He imagined the residents lounging inside, their lives steeped in luxury and ignorance. As he finished up his shift, his every step was propelled by the image of Mrs. Harper's pearl earrings, gleaming like beacons of privilege he was never afforded.

With his shift over, he reported to his supervisor over at the neighborhood clubhouse—complete with pool, tennis courts, basketball courts, and an arcade—he went to his car. There, he sank into the driver's seat, the worn fabric a stark contrast to the leather interiors that cradled the community's elite.

His hand reached under the seat, fingers brushing against metal tools, before pulling out a small velvet pouch. He loosened the drawstring, allowing the pearls within to cascade into his palm like alabaster tears. Each one held a cold fire, memories of past conquests etched into their lustrous surfaces. His thumb ran over them, feeling their smoothness, a perverse comfort.

A singular pearl caught the sunlight, reflecting it back with a soft glow. It was the first he'd taken, and it remained the standard by which he judged all others—a tangible representation of the life he'd extinguished, the power he wielded with such decisiveness.

"Mrs. Harper will make a fine addition," he mused, rolling the pearl between his fingertips. "A retired schoolteacher... living alone with no one to miss her until it's far too late."

He placed the pearls back in their pouch, tucking it away with reverence. As he pulled out of the parking lot, his hands were steady on the wheel, the leather cool and compliant beneath his grip. The rhythmic hum of the tires on asphalt was a lullaby for his roiling thoughts as he neared his own home, a paltry hovel compared to the houses he worked around.

The drive was uneventful, but within his mind, he was formulating a plan. He thought of Mrs. Harper, with her delicate hands and that garden she tended so lovingly. He imagined her surprise, the confusion that would flit across her face as the toxin took hold. It was almost enough to make him smile.

When he finally reached home, the old run-down house stood silent; once inside, he wasted no time. He headed straight for the hidden compartment behind the bookshelf, where his tools awaited their grim purpose. With clinical precision, he laid out the syringe, its contents potent enough to fell a horse. Next, another maintenance worker's uniform—pristine and pressed—to merge seamlessly into the background. And finally, the string of pearls, gleaming malevolently under the fluorescent lights.

He sat for a very long time at a lightless kitchen, hunched over the maps and layouts of the community. He traced paths with a finger, the paper rustling softly under his touch. Entrances and exits were marked, hiding spots circled with precision.

He imagined his quiet footsteps, the stealthy approach at dawn when the dew still clung to the grass, and the world held its breath in anticipation. His pulse quickened at the thought, a dark thrill coursing through him.

"Mrs. Harper," he said, his voice almost singing. "Your pearls await."

CHAPTER SEVEN

The midday sun cast an almost eerie glare on the large front windows of the Rogers residence. Once again, she and Jake were going to speak to a grieving husband. Once again, they were going to step past a threshold and enter into a house of sorrows. There was still no warrant to get into Crabtree's safe, though Tessa was beginning to think that was a small obstacle at this point—a detail that would likely come to nothing. And on the drive to the Roger's residence, Tessa had called in for an assist at the bureau, getting a team together to look for overlaps in service workers who may have passed by both the Rogers and Flowers residences in the past month.

In the meantime, Tessa thought it wise to have a closer look at the Rogers' home. They'd not yet had a chance to look it over with a keen eye, and now that they had the service worker theory hanging over them, it seemed quite important to view it afresh.

Tessa knocked on the front door, the sound cavernous and loud on the enormous front porch. The door looked like something resembling a drawbridge. When it was swung open, a woman greeted them on the other side. She was perhaps in her late thirties and looked somber. Dressed in all black and with tired eyes greeting them, Tessa assumed she was a grieving family member.

"Can I help you?" she asked.

"Yes. Agents Flint and Sullivan," Rachel said. "We were hoping we could—"

"If you're here to speak with John, he's not really up to it."

Recalling the name John Rogers from the police records, Tessa knew that he was Mary's husband—a multi-millionaire who had once been a big deal in the stock market world and was now slowly making a name for himself in the realm of social media platforms.

"Do you think he might allow us to come in and have a look around?"

The woman shrugged and, after glaring at them for a moment, simply shrugged. "I think he'd be fine with that. Come on in."

"Do you mind me asking who you are?" Jake asked.

"I'm Lacy…John's younger sister. I've been tag-teaming with our mother ever since Mary's funeral, making sure John's okay. He's sort of a mess."

"Understandably so," Tessa said.

Lacy led them through an enormous foyer and into a huge open space that Tessa supposed was supposed to serve as a living room of sorts. Tessa moved through the living room, her eyes scanning for the overlooked, the out-of-place. Jake's steady presence behind her was both a comfort and a reminder—they were a team, but it was her instincts that often peeled back the layers of deception.

"She was found in the den, correct?" Tessa asked.

"Yeah, just through there," Lacy confirmed, pointing to the left side of the living area where a tall, arched entrance led into a darkened hallway. "With a house this big, you can understand why none of the helped out here heard whatever happened."

Tessa couldn't decide if Lacy was sad about the loss of her sister-in-law or irritated about having to be here. Maybe somewhere in between.

She and Jake walked through the archway and down the hall. It emptied out into the den, another huge room that spoke of elegance and dominance. Huge paintings hung on the walls, none that Tessa recognized. The bookshelves weren't very well populated, the volumes on the shelves there mainly for looks.

An antique rolltop desk sat against the far wall. She walked over to it and slid the rolling cover-up, revealing a well-organized space beneath. The desk held stationary materials—envelopes, elegant paper, expensive pens. To the far right, there was a framed picture that had been stuffed between a container of envelopes and the side of the desk.

Tessa removed it and had a look. Mary Rogers was front and center in the picture, surrounded by four other women. They were all very pretty, dolled up for a night out. Knowing that Mary would never experience another moment like this made Tessa feel a stinging sadness, but it was quickly dashed when she noticed something in particular about what she was wearing. Not the breathtaking designer dress—though it was hard to ignore—but one of the accessories.

"Jake, have a look at this."

He hurried over, looked at the picture, and pointed to the woman in the center. "That's Mary, right?"

"Right. And do you see what she's wearing?"

With Mary frozen in a happier time, the intricacies of her pearl necklace highlighted by the flash of an unseen camera. It was identical to the one they had uncovered on Regina Flowers—a tangible link that solidified their connection. Tessa had suspected Mary was strangled by a pearl necklace from the beginning, but this provided an undeniable link.

"Seems our victims shared more than just a social circle," Jake observed. “I mean, I’m an idiot when it comes to jewelry, but that’s the same sort of necklace, right?”

“Seems like it, though it would be impossible to know for sure. Unless we can find that necklace here in the house somewhere.”

Another voice spoke up from behind them, startling both agents. “Well, you can look all you want. Have your run of the place, if you must.”

Tessa and Jake turned at the same time to see a tall, worn-down man standing in the entryway. He was wearing a black tee shirt and jeans, both loose-fitting. He held a tumbler in his right hand, filled a quarter of the way with an amber-colored liquid. The man's picture had not been included in the police report, but Tessa made an educated guess as to who he was.

“Mr. Rogers,” she said. “Lacy told us it would be okay to come in.”

“And it is. Anything I can do to help you catch the monster that took Mary from me, you just let me know.”

“Actually, there *is* something,” Jake said. “Would you happen to know where Mary kept her jewelry?”

John Rogers smiled, but there was little joy in it. “Depends on what sort of jewelry. But I think the big stuff was kept in this big, shiny box in the walk-in closet of the master bath. It’s upstairs…second room on the right.

“Thanks,” Tessa said.

She and Jake made their way out of the den, and when they started up the stairs off of the living area, she expected to turn and find John following them. But he'd done no such thing; he'd apparently retreated back into whatever hiding place he'd been in when Lacy had answered the door.

The master bedroom was roughly the size of Tessa's entire apartment. The bed was unmade, and there was a litter of dirt clothes at the foot of the bed. A box of tissues, as well as many discarded ones, sat on the floor by the bed—the remnants of a few sorrowful weeping sessions, Tessa assumed.

The master bath was to the right. It, too, was large. The shower was practically cavernous, with two faucets. There were twin sinks along a huge mirror and, as John had said, a walk-in closet. Once inside, finding the jewelry box was simple enough. It sat on top of a small table to the left of a collection of hanging clothes that Mary Roger would never wear again. The jewelry box was mahogany and had an ornate **R** carved into the top.

Tessa opened it and found a surprisingly meager amount of jewelry—though what *was* there was likely worth a small fortune. There were only two necklaces; one was gold, the other was silver, and they were both highlighted by dazzling diamonds. There were a few sets of earrings and three diamond rings, one of which was equipped with the largest diamond Tessa had ever seen outside of movies.

But there was no pearl necklace.

"If your theory is right, maybe the killer stole it?" Jack guessed.

"Maybe. But if he's stealing them, why not take Regina Flowers'?"

"Maybe hers was too well hidden. Maybe he didn't know where to look."

As they left the closet and bedroom, they met Lacy in the hallway. She was carrying a basket of dirty clothes, still wearing that hard-to-read look on her face.

"'Scuse me," she said, passing them to get into the bedroom—presumably to get the dirty clothes out of the floor.

At first, Tessa only nodded in acknowledgment and continued on her way. But out of the corner of her eye, something grabbed her attention.

"Lacy? Hold on a second, would you?"

Lacy stopped just inside the bedroom door and turned to face them. Tessa looked at the laundry basket the woman was carrying. There weren't many in there—just a few shirts and some towels from the look of it. Only, there was one other thing near the bottom, crumpled and peeking through the wide, decorative slats in the basket.

"Jake...do you see that?"

"Yeah, what is it?"

"What?" Lacy asked, now looking at the basket herself.

"Can you dump that?" Tessa asked.

Lacy looked at them as if they'd lost their minds but nodded. She dumped the dirty clothes out onto the floor and took a single step back. "Now, what is it?" she asked.

Rachel knelt down and, with a right arm that was still bandaged from their scuffle at Crabtree's, picked up the item that had caught her attention: the shirt portion of a uniform for a gardening company.

"We need to find Mr. Rogers," Tessa said. "Do you know where he escaped to?"

***

They found him in the study, a room still echoing with the ghost of normalcy—bookshelves lined with literature, an unlit fireplace, photographs gracing the walls. But there, amidst the remnants of a life interrupted, sat a man hollowed by grief. His tumbler was now empty as he sat at his desk, doing nothing…just staring blankly at the walls.

"Mr. Rogers," Tessa said, stepping into the room uninvited. "Sorry to bother you, but we do have two questions for you…two rather important questions."

"Anything if it helps find who did this to Mary," he whispered, his hands clasped tightly on his lap as though holding himself together.

"Did your wife happen to have a pearl necklace that she wore all of the time?"

"I...I think so. I mean, I know I've seen her wear pearls. But I don't know if she wore it frequently. I think it was the sort of thing she usually only broke out for special occasions. But again, as I said…I wasn't very attentive, so I could be wrong."

It wasn't the solid answer she was looking for, but it at least gave her and Jake a basic idea.

"And then the other question," Tessa said. "We noticed that Lacy was doing laundry, and there was a work uniform in it. A gardener's shirt…a button-down with a company name embroidered on the chest. I'm curious if it was yours or Mary's."

"Oh, no," John said with a shaky smile. "No, that's Joseph's."

"And who is Joseph?" Jake asked.

"A gardener, landscaper, handyman. Sort of a jack of all trades. He's been with us for years, like part of the family really."

"Was it common for him to be in your house?" Tessa asked.

"Oh, absolutely. Lunches, dinners, things like that. I'd even call him inside if he was out doing yard work for us on Saturdays if there was a particularly interesting college football game on."

"What sort of work did he do for you?"

"Like I said…landscaping and things like that. He actually did just about every single aspect of the rose garden out back. One of Mary's favorite places in the…in the house." He nearly lost control of his emotions at the end of the statement, struggling to keep it together.

"I take it with such a close bond between your family and Joseph, you trusted him completely?"

“Absolutely. I recommended him to many in the community. Everyone trusted Joseph." Mr. Rogers glanced out the window towards the once vibrant flower beds now wilting in neglect.

Tessa filed this information away next to the uniform they'd found. As she moved through the living room, she could feel the shadow of the killer lurking in the corners of the room, and it sent a shiver down her spine. The scent of fertilizer still hung faintly in the air, a ghost of routine visits by a gardener who may have known more than just which flowers needed pruning.

“If you’re going where I think you’re trying to go with this,” John said, “I can assure you that Joseph had absolutely nothing to do with Mary’s death. He was…

“Like family,” Tessa said.

“Yeah.”

Tessa offered a sympathetic smile. Her mind, however, was already racing ahead, piecing together the mosaic of Mary Rogers' life and death. “What else can you tell us about her day-to-day life?”

"Well, ever since she sort of fell out of the public eye, it's been pretty quiet. And that's been over the last year or so. She did a lot of reading, and she'd just started to track down rare copies of old children's books. A weird hobby, but it made her happy. Oh, and Thursdays were sacred—yoga in the morning, then volunteering at the community center.”

Tessa considered this, knowing that any sort of rigid routine would offer a killer a surefire way to know the ins and outs of someone's life.

“I think that’s all for now, Mr. Rogers,” Tessa said. “Thank you so much for your time.”

The silence of the Rogers' home clung to Tessa as she and Jake made their way out of the living room and back down the large hallway. As they reached the door, not escorted by either John or Lacy, Jake stopped and gestured toward the doorframe, where a sliver of black adhesive peeked from beneath the casing.

“Check that out,” he said.

"Electrician's tape," she murmured, his voice low. "Not something you'd expect to find in a place like this."

"Unless you had something to hide," Tessa replied, stepping closer to examine the anomaly. Her fingers traced the outline of the tape before pulling it back. Three wires were revealed, running along the bottom of the wall and toward the door.

“Probably to the security system,” Jake said. “There’s a camera doorbell by the door outside. So maybe the power was cut?”

"Or bypassed. This is a careful job. They did it with precision and care. They had the time to do it—from the inside. Someone knew exactly what they were doing. It wasn't brute force—it was knowledge."

"Inside job?" He pondered the implication, the weight of it settling between them.

“Perhaps.”

But without saying the name, Tessa knew that she and Jake were thinking the same thing. They were thinking of the uniform in the laundry. They were thinking of their next suspect, a man John Rogers swore was innocent.

Joseph, Tessa thought as she and Jake made their way quickly back outside.

CHAPTER EIGHT

The sun was getting lower in the sky as evening approached, casting soft shadows across the gravel of Green Thumbs Galore. It had been simple to connect Joseph to the company, as he was listed as co-owner on the website. She and Jake stepped out of the car, which Jake had parked at the front of a simple brick building beside a large stack of old planters. The building itself was quite simple, but the exterior was overflowing with flowers and plants of all kinds. Bees buzzed happily, and the smell of multiple flowers greeted them. It was a surefire way to drum up business, Tessa supposed.

"Looks peaceful enough," Jake murmured, but Tessa wasn't fooled by the serenity of the setting sun or the rustic charm of the place.

As they approached from the door—glass with a metal frame—Tessa could see a man through the window. He was standing behind a long counter, his hands busy shuffling papers as he prepared to close up shop for the day. The door chimed as they entered, and Joseph looked up, his face instantly stretching on the rehearsed smile of a small-business owner.

“Hey, folks,” he said. “If you need something quick, I can help you out. But I *am* about three minutes away from closing up shop for the day.”

"Actually, we just need to ask a few questions," Tess said. She showed her badge and I.D., stating: "We're Special Agents Flint and Sullivan. We're looking for Joseph Garcia."

“That’s me,” he said, setting the papers down and eyeing them curiously.

“Oh, good. We were hoping to ask you some questions about Mary Rogers.”

“Ah, I see.” His eyes darted to the clock on the wall, a silent wish that he was anywhere but here. "We have a few questions about your service records. Specifically, your records for the Rogers house.”

"Of course," Joseph responded, though his hands trembled ever so slightly as he opened a drawer to retrieve the documents. She observed the subtle movement, an involuntary twitch that betrayed his nerves. Tessa's gut tightened; there was something amiss here.

Jake leaned against the counter, watching Joseph intently as he handed over the records. "How long had you been working on their property?"

"A little over two years, I suppose. And...well, it's because of John and Mary that I've done as well as I have. They really spread the word for me when I was starting out."

"Do you recall what the first job you took for them was?" Jake asked as he started flipping through the service reports and invoices.

"Basic weeding, believe it or not. Mary had it in her head that they were going to have a gorgeous flower bed out front, but the weeds were a nightmare. So they hired me. And I made some suggestions they liked, and they kept hiring me for other small stuff. When they found out I was also a handyman, they kept me *very* busy."

As he spoke, Tessa caught the faintest sheen of sweat on his brow despite the coolness of the office. Her detective instincts hummed like live wires—why was he nervous if he had nothing to hide?

"Joseph, we're just trying to piece together her last few days," Tessa said, softening her voice in an attempt to coax him into openness. And then she'd hit him with the details about his work outfit and the electrical tape near the door. "Any detail, no matter how small, could be crucial."

"For me? Nothing out of the ordinary," he said quickly, too quickly. Tessa exchanged a glance with Jake, who gave a nearly imperceptible nod. They both sensed the discordance in Joseph's demeanor, the unsung notes of distress that hung in the air like the fragrance of the flowers outside.

Tessa's gaze was unyielding as she watched Joseph's hands, which seemed to dance with a nervous energy of their own. Each time he reached for the stack of service records on his cluttered desk, his fingers twitched, betraying an inner unrest. The papers seemed to quake slightly under his touch, and the tremor in his voice when he spoke did little to reassure.

"When were you last at the Roger's residence?" she asked.

"About a week ago. Maybe a bit more. Nine days at most."

"And what was the purpose of that visit?"

He gently took the stack of records from Jake and pulled one out. He handed it to Tessa and as she looked it over, he said, "One of the sprinklers out in the rose garden had a clog in it. I went out to fix it and ended up also putting some more mulch down."

Across from her, Jake continued to study the documents. He was the picture of focus, the set of his jaw speaking volumes about his determination to unearth any discrepancies.

"Joseph," Tessa said, "how well did you know Mary Rogers?"

At this question, something crumpled in Joseph's posture. His eyes, which had so adamantly refused to meet theirs, now glistened with a sheen of sudden grief. "Mrs. Rogers... Mary was kind to me," he stammered, his voice thick with emotion. "She didn't treat me like... like I was just the help. She and John both treated me like family. And it's a horrible, horrible thing that she was killed."

"Did her death come as a shock to you?" Jake interjected, still sifting through paperwork but watching Joseph closely.

"Of course," Joseph whispered, his voice nearly lost in the hum of the fan. "She was always so... so full of life. It doesn't seem real that she's gone."

Tessa's gut twisted with a cocktail of emotions—frustration, empathy, and the relentless drive for answers. She had seen grief before, raw and unforgiving, and there was no mistaking its bitter grasp in Joseph's demeanor. Despite the gnawing suspicion that had drawn them to his doorstep, the sorrow etched into his features seemed genuine, untainted by guilt or subterfuge.

"Can you tell us about your interactions you had with her in the past month or so?"

His fingers trailed along the grain of the wooden table, leaving smudges on its surface. "Mary... she was kind. Always asked about my family," he said, hesitantly meeting her gaze before it slipped away again. "I can't remember anything unusual. I just did my job, tended the garden. She'd talk about books she'd read, drama on social media, that sort of thing. But there wasn't anything different or unusual the last few times we spoke."

"Did she seem worried or mention any concerns?" Jake chimed in, flipping through his notes.

"No, not that I recall," Joseph replied, his voice trailing off into a whisper.

"So why don't you tell us how one of your shirts ended up in the Roger's laundry?" She dropped the question like a bomb on the counter.

He smiled almost fondly. "That day I went to check the clog in the line and put the mulch down, the nozzle head got away from me. I slipped right in that new mulch, and I got soaked…and filthy. John insisted I come in and change…gave me a shirt to change into and everything."

Tessa leaned forward, scrutinizing his face for any tell-tale signs of deceit. But there were none. Besides, the story would be easy enough to check with John Rogers.

"As we were leaving their house today," Jake said, "we noticed some black electrical tape right at the front door…really low, near the baseboards. We peeled it aside and saw that there were three exposed wires. Looked like they were attached to that front doorbell. Do you know anything about that?"

"I do. It's the one job I've never been able to completely fix. Most of those electronic, camera-based doorbells run on batteries, but some of the more expensive ones can be hardwired right into the house. I installed that thing for them earlier this year, and it keeps glitching. I tried fixing it, checking the wiring through the hole you found under the tape, but was never able to."

"So why leave the tape there?" Jake pressed.

"I told Mary that I wouldn't be offended if they hired an actual electrician to fix it. I left the tape there for easy access to whoever ended up coming to fix the doorbell." He eyed them with a bit of hurt in his expression and said, "If you're trying to figure out if I had something to do with Mary's murder, I had *nothing* to do with it. I'd never hurt Mary or John."

"I'm beginning to believe that," Tessa said.

"All the same, is there anyone who can vouch for your whereabouts on the nights of the murders?" Jake asked, his tone even but insistent.

"Murders? As in more than one? My goodness…"

"Yes, another one," Tessa said. "Have you ever heard any negative talk from your fellow workers? Maybe something hostile or threatening about a client?"

"Sort of. But it's never anything serious, you know? Some people in my line of work get bitter and jealous of all these rich folks who hire us. But it's just trash-talking, you know?"

"A woman was murdered in the same fashion as Mary Rogers just last night. Any chance you know a woman named Regina Flowers?"

Joseph thought it over for a moment but ultimately shook his head. "The last name *Flowers* sounds familiar, but I don't know a Regina Flowers. As for your other question about people who can verify where I've been the last few nights, there's my wife, for starters. I can give you her number."

He was so willingly offering up information that Tessa felt the trail growing cold with each passing second. Their questioning continued, delving into the mundane aspects Joseph's private life—his routine trips to the hardware store, quiet dinners and TV-binging with his wife at night. There was nothing that painted him in a suspicious light, nothing that connected him to the victims beyond his professional capacity.

Despite the anomaly of the electrical tape and the abandoned uniform, Tessa struggled to make the pieces fit into the framework of guilt. She looked down to her bandaged arm, the injury almost completely forgotten, frustrated by the lack of hard evidence. Her instincts honed from years on the force screamed that something was amiss, yet Joseph wasn't a marker along that particular path.

"Thank you for your cooperation, Joseph," Tessa finally said, signaling to Jake that it was time to leave.

Back in the car, as Jake backed out of the lot, Tessa did her best not to feel discouraged. Her gut told her Joseph was innocent, but she also recalled his jittery movements, the way his eyes darted away from direct questions, the nervous energy that seemed to emanate from him.

"Let's not close the book on Joseph yet," she stated, the decision firm in her voice despite the uncertainty that gnawed at her. "I doubt he's our killer, but he may be an associate or peer of whoever it is. The gardener and handyman route is still a promising one."

"Agreed," Jake nodded, pushing off from the vehicle. "We keep an eye on him—surveillance, check his financials, see who he talks to. Maybe he'll lead us somewhere without realizing."

Tessa settled into the passenger seat, her gaze fixed on the road ahead as it led them to the end of the day…and without a suitable lead.

Still, something Joseph had said stuck with her, itching at her instincts. *"Some people in my line of work get bitter and jealous of all these rich folks that hire us.."*

Tessa was beginning to see how that might be true…and how it might become strong enough to drive someone to very horrible deeds.

CHAPTER NINE

The setting sun painted the sky over the rocky coast in melancholy purples and oranges. But the beauty of it was lost on her as she pulled her car into the driveway of her home. On the porch, she fumbled with her keys, her mind still racing from the day's seemingly fruitless searching. She stepped into the solitude of her home, shedding her professional armor with each layer of clothing she peeled away.

She instantly walked to her bedroom, where she swapped her tailored suit for a worn sweater and jeans. Even at home, she forced herself into routine. Form the bedroom, she wasted no time in going to the kitchen to prepare a hot, home-cooked meal. The methodical chopping of vegetables and the sizzle of browning meat briefly grounded her in the moment.

She turned the burner down to a simmer before retreating to her library. Surrounded by shelves of well-loved books, Tessa collapsed into an overstuffed armchair, a random novel plucked from the collection clutched in her hands. She tried to lose herself in its pages, to let fiction erase reality, if only for a moment.

But reality clawed back, dragging her thoughts to pearl necklaces. And just like that, she knew it was going to be *that* sort of case—the sort that sank its claws in and never let go until it was solved. With a sigh, she closed the book, its plot already forgotten, and picked up the case files once more. She carried them into the kitchen and set them on the small dining table in the corner. Moments later, she had her dinner and a glass of wine with the files, reading them as she ate.

"Two women, two necklaces, no connection…" she spoke out loud into the empty house. Her voice trailed off as she spread out the photos and reports like a macabre puzzle. It was as she pored over the details – the demographics, the locations, the timelines – that a shiver ran down her spine, an echo from the past whispering through the recesses of her memory.

This time, it went deeper than the memories of doctor's visits concerning her condition. This time, it was about her sister.

Sarah, she thought. She nearly spoke her name out loud, but the mere idea of doing so felt almost sacrilegious.

Sarah had vanished one summer night, leaving behind nothing but an empty room and a family forever fractured. The only clue had been a removed screen from the outside of the house, giving access to the window to Sarah's room. No fingerprints and no other clues. A dead, cold case.

Tessa's pulse quickened as pieces fell into place; not of the case—not exactly—but of her drive to solve it. Of her drive to capture every dark shadow out there who might do harm to the innocent.

She was still trying to find Sarah. She was still trying to make sense of what had happened, making a move to do it case by case. As for this case, she saw women on the cusp of life, suddenly and violently ripped from this world.

Secretly, had she been subconsciously seeing Sarah's face in every crime scene photo she'd ever seen? It was striking in that moment, looking at photos of Mary Rogers and Regina Flowers. Only, she saw Sarah at the age of fourteen—the last time she'd ever seen her sister. She remembered the pajamas she'd been wearing, the smell of her toothpaste as they'd giggled about something in the hallway of their Bangor home just before bed.

Sarah had surfaced like a whale breaking the sea in her mind and she knew it wasn't going anywhere. This was even dwarfing memories of doctors' offices and broken limbs and scrapes that she never felt.

Before she was fully aware of what she was doing, Tessa reached for her phone. She pulled up a number she'd not dialed since Christmas—nearly seven months ago. Her finger hovered over it for a moment before she pressed call. She exhaled slowly, steadying her nerves before dialing the familiar number that still etched itself into her memory. She didn't want to make the call; in fact, she'd be fine never making it again for the remainder of her life.

But if she was truly going to dig into Sarah's case, it was a call she'd eventually have to make. So she may as well do it now while she felt at least somewhat confident.

The phone rang once, and she saw Sarah's face.

It rang twice, and she saw the broken, slightly ripped screen window from Sarah's room.

The call was answered in the third ring. "Hello?" answered a gruff voice.

"Hey, Dad. It's Tessa." She tried to inject warmth into her words, a balm to soothe the months of silence between them. And beyond those months of silence, at least five years of anger and tension.

"Well…hey," he replied, a shade softer. "To what do I owe the pleasure?"

"Nothing much. Just wanted to check in. How's the boat coming along?" Tessa asked, picturing the old fishing vessel he'd been restoring—an attempt at finding solace in retirement.

"Fighting me every step of the way. But she'll sail again." There was a pride in his voice that she rarely heard.

"That's great, Dad," Tessa responded, her voice genuine despite the tightness in her chest. It hadn't felt natural to talk to him in a while…as far back as when Darah had disappeared six years ago.

"Tessa…don't get me wrong…I love hearing from you. But did you really call to just chew the fat? To ask me about a boat I've been tinkering with for a few years?"

She appreciated his directness. He'd always been that way, both as a father and a husband. His wife—Tessa's mom—had died when Tessa was ten and Sarah was six. But Tessa had seen enough of his interactions with her mother to know the kind of husband he'd been.

"Ah, you got me," she said flatly.

"So spill. What is it?"

"Dad," she began, hesitancy threading her tone, "I've been working on a case. And... it's brought up some things. About Sarah. Not the case itself…I think just the chase of it."

There was a pause, and she imagined him retreating behind his hardened exterior, the father who had lost as much as she had but never dared to show it.

"What about Sarah?" His voice was cautious, a sentinel guarding against the resurgence of old pain.

"It's hard to explain, but I'm just realizing that a lot of my…of my *fire* behind what I do what I do stems from losing her. From not having answers."

"Well, shit, Tess…why would you do that to yourself? That case is cold and we…we aren't ever going to have the answers you're looking for."

She ignored the jab, determined to get this out. "I feel like wanting answers to her disappearance keeps me an honest agent…keeps my mind sharp. And almost daily, whether I want to admit it or not, I keep wondering if we missed something. Us, the police, whoever. What if..."

"Enough, Tessa," he cut in, his tone bristling with a mixture of concern and weariness. "That road only leads to more heartache. You know we turned over every stone. Some of them several times."

"I know, Dad, but—"

"Let it lie, Tessie. For your own sake," he interjected, a finality in his voice that brooked no argument.

She knew he was getting defensive because he'd been a member of the police force who had failed to find her. He was feeling attacked. *Good,* she thought. *Screw him.*

"I can't leave alone," she said. "You know that."

"Oh, I know. It's that FBI in you. Always needing to prove something."

His words stung, carrying with them the weight of unspoken disappointment. She could almost see him leaning back in his chair, the lines on his forehead deepening with each word of veiled criticism.

"Still pissed about my choices?" Tessa's voice hardened, her investigator's instincts honing in on the subtext. "Or is it easier to point fingers at me than to face the fact that we never found out what happened to Sarah?"

She heard him sigh, and she knew what was coming next. She'd said too much, been too hard on him. But her investigator's mind, once hooked, could not let go. Especially not when she was dealing with a case where two innocent women had been killed, and she had no leads.

"Take care of yourself," he said. It was his not-so-subtle way of saying he had no interest in talking about this. Or any interest at all in simply talking *to her.*

"I always do," she replied, ending the call with a sed of anger pulsing in her heart. And then, with the call over, she muttered: "You bastard."

Tessa leaned back in her chair, the silence of the house wrapping around her like a shroud. Her father's words echoed in her mind, a chorus of warning and fear, but they could not drown out the whisper of possibility that nagged at her. Sarah's face, younger and brighter than the victims in the photographs but hauntingly similar, stared back at her from the depths of memory.

On the table before her lay the files, the photos, the notes—all pieces of a puzzle that refused to fit together. A puzzle that, in some twisted way, seemed interlocked with the one piece of her past she could never find. With Sarah still on her mind, Tessa looked to her bandaged arm. Slowly, she took the bandages off. She needed to clean the wounds again; she'd do it after dinner. But, as she usually did whenever she received a wound of this kind, she found herself probing it.

She poked at it with her fingers, even pulled the akin down a bit to aggravate the cuts places there by Crabtree's glass. But of course, no matter what she did, there was no pain.

She finished eating and took her plate to the sink, placing it in with the other dirty dishes from dinner. She then made her way to the bathroom, where she figured she'd properly wash the cuts before allowing herself a nice, long bath.

However, just as she made these plans, her cell phone rang as she stepped into the bathroom. Only fifteen minutes had passed since the call with her father. She wondered if it was him calling four Round Two. He did that sometimes.

She was so sure it was him that she didn't even check the caller display. "Hello?"

"There's been another one, Tessa," Jake's voice said on the other end. "How soon can you be in town?"

Images of her father disintegrated at the comment…at Jake's voice. Adrenaline surged as she sprang from her seat, the specters of the past fueling her determination. There was no time for rest, no space for personal demons. The pearl necklace killer had struck again.

"Where?"

"Harborview Park."

"Give me twenty minutes," she said.

CHAPTER TEN

The grandeur of yet another high-end neighborhood loomed over Tessa, a stark contrast to the grim task at hand. She stepped out of her car (she'd come straight from home so it was her car, not the usual bureau sedan), her eyes tracing the elegant lines of the house that stood before her in the waning light—a beautiful facade hiding the ugliness within. As she approached the threshold, she could feel the weight of her badge against her chest, a constant reminder of the oath she'd taken to pursue justice, no matter how dark the path.

She spotted Jake on the porch, speaking with two cops. As Tessa approached them, a third man came out—a man she didn't know personally but had seen at a number of crime scenes. His last name was Ritcher, and he was a member of a local forensics unit.

All three men gave Tessa nods and acknowledgment as she came up the stairs into the large, tiled porch. The porch light hanging over her head cast an eerie glow like an opulent spaceship.

"I'm all done in there," Ritcher said, barely pausing a beat before making his way down the stairs to the sidewalk. "Help yourself, agents."

Jake shrugged at Tessa and said, "Shall we?"

He pushed open the door with a gloved hand, and they entered the house.

The moment Tessa crossed into the living room, the familiar scent of death greeted her, metallic and invasive. It wasn't something she'd smelled when she first started as an agent, but now it was hard to *not* notice it after just three years as an agent.

Jake led the way through a semicircle-shaped foyer and down a stunted hallway that opened up on the left, revealing the kitchen. Her pulse quickened, and she forced herself to look at the body lying on the floor. The woman lay sprawled between the counter and a large farmhouse-style table, her lifeless eyes staring into nothingness. She was considerably older than the other two victims, somewhere north of sixty, if Tessa had to guess.

A pearl necklace was clasped around her neck, each bead reflecting the expensive hanging lights over the bar area behind her.

"Same M.O.," Tessa observed, her voice steady despite the chill that tickled her spine. "The pearls...they're becoming his calling card. What's her name?"

“Edith Harper.”

“Age?”

“Not sure. I think one of the cops out front said sixty-seven.”

Jake knelt by the body with clinical detachment. "We should check for the signs." His gloved fingers traced the victim’s wrists, lifting them gently. "See here?" he pointed out, his words directed more at himself than at Tessa. "Subcutaneous hemorrhaging. She tried to fight back."

Tessa nodded as she looked to the woman’s neck, her hands also covered with latex gloves. Like the others, the indentation of a necklace was hard to miss. The marks around Edith Harper’s neck were an angry red, fresh and punctuated with light scratch marks.

“Who found her?” Tessa asked.

“Ah, the police, actually. Apparently, a silent alarm was triggered at some point during the killer’s visit. She’s not been dead for long. Maybe an hour and a half at most.”

Her mind raced, threading through every detail of the previous cases, looking for something they might have missed, something that could lead them to the person who had done this.

"Three murders, Jake. Three lives snuffed out, and all we have are these damned pearls." Tessa's hands balled into fists, frustration searing through her veins. She hated feeling helpless, hated the slow, creeping fear that they were always one step behind.

"Let's canvass the room place," he proposed. "There has to be something more, something we're not seeing. Maybe something forensics overlooked."

As they combed through the room, Tessa's mind churned with thoughts of her sister—another unsolved mystery that clawed at her heart. Those thoughts, plus this maddening case, created an empty feeling within her, a hollow of sorts that her heart was falling into.

"Each victim rich, alone, and now adorned with these pearls," she breathed out, a trail of logic beginning to form. "What does he want us to see?"

“Rogers and Flowers were married,” Jake said. “Our latest victim, Ms. Edith Harper, was single. That’s the only difference I can come up with right now.”

They lapsed into silence, each turning in their own direction as they continued to look the kitchen area over for a clue that was gone unseen. Tessa recalled the pearl they’d found at the Flowers residence all alone and on the carpet. She crouched low, her shadow merging with the dark shapes cast by the dining table, chairs, and the stools around the bar. The light from above was harsh, almost clinical. She looked in the bit of space beneath the space under the counters, under the table, under each chair…but nothing.

As she turned and faced in the direction of the refrigerator, though, she thought she saw something. She crawled closer but saw only grime and a collection of dust bunnies beneath the fridge. She withdrew her phone and switched on the flashlight feature. Aiming it under the fridge, her heart leapt with excitement.

"Found something," she said.

"Under the fridge?" Jake asked, walking over.

"Yeah." She did her best to slip her hand under the bulky shape, but there was resistance at her wrist. She pushed harder, trying to wedge it in far beyond the point most people would have pulled away out of discomfort. This was one of those times where the inability to feel pain was quite helpful. Still, what she'd seen was just barely out of her reach.

"Can you lift it up just a bit?" she asked Jake.

"Yeah, but Jesus, Tessa. Don't break your arm trying to get under there."

She ignored the comment and waited for him to lift. When he did, she moved her hand closer and grabbed the object she'd spotted. A small sphere rolled under her probing gaze—a pearl, lustrous but visibly out of place.

"I wonder how long that's been under there," Jake said.

"Not long at all," Tessa said. "It's still got its luster. If it had been under there for a decent amount of time, it would be dull. And the dust would have stuck to it. This pearl was intentionally placed under there. And recently."

"You're sure?"

She shrugged as she got to her feet. "Maybe not one hundred percent, but…yeah, sure enough."

She observed the pearl closely, and even though she was no jewelry expert, she could see differences between this pearl and the one they'd found at the Flowers residence. This one had a unique iridescence, a subtle hue distinctly unlike the creamy string adorning the victim's neck.

"This pearl also doesn't match the one on Ms. Harper's neck," Tessa pointed out.

Jake was already reaching into the inside pocket of his overcoat. "Let's bag it," he said. "Looks like another trip to the labs, huh?"

"Looks like it."

As Tessa slid the pearl into an evidence pouch, a faint scent teased her nostrils. It was slight but noticeable—like a cleaning agent of some kind. It was a harsh smell, though, not sweet and perfumed.

"So you smell that?" she asked.

"I did when I first came in," Jake said. "Bleach, maybe?"

"More like chlorine, I think." She sniffed again, more deliberately, and there it was—a clean, chemical tang.

Jake sniffed the air and nodded in agreement. "Yeah, that's exactly what it is."

"Is there a pool out back?"

"No idea. But even so, why would we smell it *here* if there is? Hold on, I'll check."

As Jake headed out, Tessa had a quick look around the rest of the house. The living room was immaculately clean. There were two paintings on the wall, both of abstract flowers. She also noted that there were two vases of roses in the living room. Tessa sniffed at them, finding them fresh; they'd not come from a florist or grocer. There was likely a rose bush somewhere nearby that she'd taken them from.

A further inspection of the living room, hallway, and bedroom revealed that Ms. Harper was a retired school teacher. She had several cards on her mantle and bedroom dresser from the students and faculty of a local middle school.

As she made her way back to the living room, Jake was coming in through the garage door at the back of the house. "No pool," he said. "And I checked the garage *and* laundry room on my way out. No chlorine or anything that could be mistaken for it. There *is* a jug of bleach under the laundry room sink, but it's closed."

"Strange." The sense of foreboding that had settled over her since entering the crime scene deepened, wrapping around her like the evening fog that clung to the streets outside. This case was a puzzle with pieces that refused to fit neatly together, and time was slipping away. Toss in her assault on personal memories, and it had been a heavy day, to say the least.

"Here's a plan," Jack said. "I'll stick around here and wait for the coroner…see if I can figure out where the hell that smell is coming from and if it had anything to do with the murder. You hit up the lab and see what you come up with. Your last visit there got us a lead, after all."

“One that led to a dead-end.”

“And some nasty cuts,” Jake pointed out, nodding to her right arm.

With one last glance at each other, they parted ways—Jake remaining in the house among local law enforcement while returning to the FBI lab's mineralogy division.

As she drove, the city lights streaked past in blurs of amber and red. With her phone connected to the car's Bluetooth system, and she dialed up Special Agent in Charge Lawson. She knew if she didn’t do it now, before it got too late, it would slip her mind and Lawson would ream her for a lack of updates in the morning.

"Flint," Lawson's gravelly voice answered after two rings. “How are you?”

"You know about the third murder, I assume?”

“I do.”

“We found another unique pearl, separate from the necklace found on the victim. I’m headed to the lab to get it tested.”

"Anything else?" Oddly, Lawson's direct approach to almost everything reminded Tessa of her father. She'd always assumed it was one of the reasons it was so difficult for them to get along.

"Nothing. Though we did smell chlorine on the scene, and we were unable to trace it."

“No pool?”

“No.”

"Chlorine..." Lawson mused, a thoughtful pause stretching between them. "Tell me...what's your read, Flint?"

Tessa exhaled slowly, her breath fogging the windshield momentarily. "The murders are escalating, becoming more frequent. This killer is meticulous, leaving us breadcrumbs seemingly on purpose, but we're always a step behind."

"Understood. Get that pearl analyzed ASAP. This could be the break we need."

"I’m almost there," Tessa confirmed before ending the call.

The car was silent again, and when the memories of Sarah tried once again to break the surface of her mind, Tessa forced them away with considerable mental effort. It was just her and the night…and another damned pearl that she hoped might burst open with some form of truth.

***

The drive to the lab was a blur of streetlights and shadowy figures, each moment propelling Tessa closer to the answers that seemed to dance just beyond her grasp. She continued to fight away the push of memories from her past, and though she was able to do so, she knew she'd have to do something about it after the case—a meeting with a psychiatrist, perhaps. Or maybe, *finally*, an actual heart-to-heart talk with her father.

Such ideas seemed to blur time, and before she knew it, the lab loomed ahead. She parked and strode toward the building, the bagged pearl in hand, hoping it might somehow bring them closer to their monster.

Having been there yesterday, Tessa felt like she was literally retracing her steps. Being so late—nearly 10:00 by now, there was no one else navigating the halls. However, just like the night before, Dr. Lucas Carter was again waiting within the lab's central hub.

"Another pearl?" he asked, eyeing the small evidence bag in her hand.

"Yes, but this one is different than the previous one. Even my untrained eye can see that."

Lucas nodded, sensing the urgency of her request. He waved her over toward another workstation and took the evidence bag from her. With gloved hands, he plucked the pearl out and placed it on the slide beneath the lens.

Tessa leaned in, her breath held hostage by the possibility of revelation. The machine hummed to life, its inner workings probing the object for the secrets it might yield.

It took less than three seconds for Lucas to let out a *"hmmm."*

"What is it?" Tessa asked.

"Forgive me for asking because I am *not* an agent on your level, but…was this dusted for prints?"

"No. I wanted to find out more about the pearl itself and…ah, hell." She wouldn't say that she'd made a mistake, because other agents would have also prioritized a trip to the lab over checking for prints—especially given there had been no prints from the first two scenes. But in this case, she'd simply made the wrong call…something that didn't happen very often.

"There's a partial print here," Lucas said. "More than partial, actually. It's faint, but it's something." His fingers danced across the keyboard, enhancing the image until the whorls and ridges of a fingerprint emerged like a ghost from the past.

"You can run fingerprint analysis here, right?" Tessa asked, her pulse quickening with each pixel of evidence materializing before her eyes.

"Well, the mineralogy department isn't quite set up for it, but..." He stopped and smiled, opening up a bit of software on the laptop and signing in. "We do, from time to time, pull prints off of things like rocks and bricks. Sometimes, the oils that are often found in fingerprints absorb certain minerals in a different way. So...yes, I can run it for you. Give me just a second."

Tessa could almost hear the tick of the clock growing louder, each second bloating with potential. The screen blinked once, twice, looking through the database. It wasn't the exact same system they used at the Portland field office, but it was very similar. While they waited, Lucas went back to the microscope, giving this new pearl the same level of scrutiny he'd given the previous one.

However, he didn't have much time to look. Less than a minute later, the fingerprint database provided a result. Usually, with partial prints, databases would end up giving a few options—as many as four or five at times. But this print was whole enough to provide them with just a single, resolute match.

David Benson, age forty-six, a Portland native. His last known address was less than twenty minutes from the lab. But more importantly, about ten from Harborview Park, where Edith Harper had been killed in her home.

Tessa felt a grim satisfaction clamp around her heart. They had a real lead at last.

"Good work, Dr. Carter."

Lucas shrugged. "The software did all the work. But now *I'll* get to work on analyzing this pearl. I'll send the data through email when I'm done."

"Perfect."

As Tessa strode away, her thoughts churned with the implications of their find. They had been grasping at shadows, chasing echoes in the darkness, but now... now they had a tangible thread to pull. The predator who had slipped through their fingers time and again was finally within reach. They had a face, a name, and an address.

Sarah's face flashed in her mind, as did that damned broken screen window—a reminder of why she pursued justice with such ferocity. This time, Tessa vowed, there would be no escape. David Benson's anonymity had been stripped away, and the end of this case was within sight.

And if Tessa had anything to say about it, his reign of terror would be over within the hour.

CHAPTER ELEVEN

The neighborhood was the sort where children's chalk art still decorated the sidewalks, and neighbors waved to each other from their porches. Economically, it was several rungs down from the exclusive neighborhoods and estates they'd visited so far for this case, but it was also far from lower class. It was quaint and charming, even as the clock inched closer to midnight. But as Tessa surveyed David Benson's unassuming home, a shiver crept along her spine. It was the perfect kind of neighborhood to hide dark secrets and plans.

Tessa had driven this time, picking Jake up from the precinct where he'd been working with the cops to get a better understanding of the crime scene. There was still no clear answer to the scent of chlorine.

"You good to go?" Tessa asked.

Jake nodded. They both knew it was always a risky bet to knock on a door at such a late hour—especially when they knew next to nothing about the person on the other side. The criminal database revealed that to date, the only ding on David Benson's record were two speeding tickets and a bar fight at the age of twenty-two.

Jake took the lead and stepped up onto the porch. He knocked with urgency as Tessa stayed a few steps back, ready for anything.

Surprisingly, they got a response almost right away. Quick, shuffling footsteps approached from the other side of the door. A man's voice called out: "Who's there? You know how late it is, right?"

"We're with the FBI," Jake said. "We need to have a word."

There was a brief silence, but then the sound of a lock being unlatched broke it. The door opened a few inches, and David Benson looked out. He was much older than the picture that had popped up in the database, but it was unmistakably him. A bushy beard hung from his chin, beginning to go gray. Long, deep crow's feet extended outward from his brown eyes.

"FBI?" he asked. "What for?"

"We need to ask you some questions," Tessa said, showing her badge and I.D. "Could we come inside?"

Benson thought about this for a moment and then shook his head. "Nah. I don't think so. It's late, and I don't have any idea why the FBI would even be here. I don't—"

Tessa acted without thinking—which was *very* unlike her. She took two huge strides forward and pushed her way inside. Benson stumbled back a bit, so shocked by the sudden movement that he didn't even think to try pushing the door closed against her.

"Hey, what the hell?" Benson said. "You can't just barge in!"

He was right, but Tessa wasn't about to tell him that. She turned to Jake and saw that he was standing in the doorway, uncertain of what to do. is look of confusion in his eyes echoed Benson's initial response. *What the hell, Tessa?*

But it was too late now. They were inside and Tessa was already taking a look around the living room that opened up off of the front door.

The house was meticulously organized, almost obsessively so. The air seemed to grow heavy, charged with an unsettling energy. A laptop was opened on the coffee table, a can of energy drink beside it. Tessa walked in that direction and glanced to the laptop.

An involuntary gasp escaped Tessa's lips. "Jake…"

Jake finally stepped inside, clearly uneasy about doing so. At the same time, Benson took a step toward the coffee table, looking back and forth between the agents like a trapped animal.

As Jake joined her by the laptop, they both looked to the screen. Apparently, just before they'd arrived, David Benson had been looking at Edith Harper's Facebook profile. With the print on the pearl discovered in her house, there was no way it was a coincidence.

"Do you know Ms. Harper?" Tessa asked.

Benson shook his head. His eyes were darting back and forth, a man looking for a way out. Second by second, Tessa could practically smell the guilt coming off of him.

"No?" Jake asked. "So why are you on her Facebook profile?"

"Is that…is that a crime?"

"No, but it *is* suspicious when we've just come from her house…where she'd recently been killed," Tessa said.

"No, see, I…"

"We found a pearl under her refrigerator, Mr. Benson," Tessa said. Her nerves and muscles were tight, her body ready for anything. "And it had your fingerprint on it."

"My finger…my…ah, Christ…no, you don't understand."

"Then explain," Jake demanded, stepping closer to him.

But Benson instead chose to kick the coffee table. It went flipping upward, the laptop crashing against the couch. In a rebound move, Benson bolted, throwing a shoulder into Jack, who was still confounded by what had happened to the coffee table. Tessa watched as Jake reached out for him, trying to catch Benson, but only his fingertips managed to grab at Benson's shoulder as Jake fought for balance. By the time Tessa and Jake were fully aware of just what was happening, Benson was already at the door.

"That's a mistake!" Tessa called out, going for her holstered Glock.

But Benson kept moving, rushing out onto the porch and out into the night. He slammed the door behind him, a lazy yet effective obstacle.

Adrenaline surged through Tessa's as she gave chase. The front door slammed open, and Tessa went sprinting down the driveway, with Jake trailing after her. Benson was just a murky shape, a shadow among the glowering street lights, his desperate footsteps pounding against the pavement.

"Stop! FBI!" Tessa shouted, but Benson was weaving through the neighboring yards now, a desperate animal fleeing the hunt.

"Split up!" Jake yelled as they reached the street. His voice sounded louder than it actually was in the suburban silence. Most of these people were asleep, settling down for another day of work and responsibilities tomorrow.

Tessa veered left and into a dark side yard, her eyes locked on the fleeing figure. She could hear her own breaths, feel her heart hammering as she ran alongside a house with an extended back deck. She pushed harder, her long strides eating up the distance between them.

"Give it up!" she barked, catching a glimpse of Benson's panicked face as he risked a look back.

They careened past picket fences and garden gnomes, past a few startled faces peering out of windows. This was not how she had envisioned the confrontation, but now there was no turning back. If she lost him now, the answers they so desperately needed might slip away forever.

She would catch him. She had to. Even as he came to the end of the block and crossed the street into more yards, she was determined not to let him out of her sight. She kept looking to her left, among the openings between houses, looking to see if Jake was angling in, but there was no sight of him.

After three more houses, Benson turned right, entering into a tangle of thin trees and underbrush. It all looked tangled and abstract in the darkness, but Tessa followed just the same. The mess only went on for several yards before it emptied out a partially developed, paved lot. There, Benson's figure flickered in and out of view as he darted between dumpsters and leaped over obstacles no more than twenty feet ahead of her.

"Stop!" she commanded, her voice echoing off the brick walls, but it only seemed to spur him on faster. She drew her Glock, not wanting to fire unless absolutely necessary but willing to do it.

Tessa's mind worked in tandem with her limbs, calculating distances, gauging his speed, her training kicking in where words failed. Each turn he took, she predicted; every shortcut he sought, she countered. She felt the rhythm of the chase thrumming in her veins, a testament to countless hours spent honing her instincts until they were razor-sharp.

The paved lot gave way to a more defined construction site. It loomed ahead, its skeleton of steel beams a stark contrast against the sky. Benson made for it without hesitation, likely in search of a hiding spot. Tessa followed, feeling the familiar burn in her muscles but also a strange exhilaration. This was where she excelled, where she left no room for doubt or debate. Even if her muscles began to protest, she'd not feel it. Of course, the downside was that she could overextend herself and not even realize it until her body simply collapsed. It had only happened twice during the course of her career, and she was learning to get a better sense for it.

She watched as his shadowy figure clambered up a set of concrete stairs that led to the second floor of a soon-to-be building without walls. She followed him right away, the obstacle back-firing on him as she was able to use it to shorten the space between them. At the top, amid stacks of concrete blocks and the hum of distant machinery, Benson turned, eyes wild. He lunged at her, and Tessa didn't see the length of the rebar until it was too late.

Tessa reacted instinctively, blocking the blow with her forearm, feeling the impact reverberate through bone yet registering no pain. It would bruise, and she may have a cracked forearm, but that was an issue for later.

With her Glock still held in her hand, she delivered a fierce right-handed blow. It cracked him along the left side of the face, and he spun in a half-circle. She could see the whites of his eyes, the beads of sweat mingling with dirt on his brow. He was panting, frenetic energy giving way to the dawning realization of defeat.

"If you try running again, I *will* shoot you," she said. "But just in the knee. Nothing fatal. Still…I'm told it hurts like a bitch."

She heard footfalls hurrying along down below. "Flint?" Jake called out, remembering to use her last name in a situation like this despite the adrenaline and thrill of the chase.

"I'm good. We're up here."

She could see Benson trying to decide if he could make a run for it. There were unfinished hallways behind him and certainly a drop back down to the ground somewhere. But then Jake was there, already taking in the scene and reaching for his handcuffs.

"Mr. Benson, I *do not* like to run," Jake said. "But that's not why you're under arrest."

With Tessa still holding him at gunpoint, Jake cuffed David Benson and began to read him his rights. Tessa holstered her gun and took a moment to look at her right arm—the one she'd used to block the rebar attack. That arm had had a tough day, first cut up by glass from a jewelry display case (and still bandaged from it) and then a pretty good whack with rebar.

X-rays in my future, she thought sadly.

"You good?" Jake asked her as he cinched the cuffs in tighter on Benson.

"Yeah. He got me pretty good with a chunk of rebar." She approached Benson and looked him in the eyes. "So *now,* do you want to explain yourself?"

Benson responded by tilting his head back slightly and spitting in her face.

Tessa wiped it away and took a few steps back, afraid of how she might react. "I'm going to call this in," she said. "I think it's smarter that the P.D. takes him away. If I put him in a car with me right now, I might kill the bastard."

"Good call," Jake said. There was worry in his voice and he was looking at her with concern.

She understood the concern. She'd barged into Benson's house (which she was starting to fear might come back to bite them), had just wrapped up an exhausting foot chase, and had it all capped off with a potential murderer spitting in her face.

It was shaping up to be one hell of a night, and it wasn't over yet.

***

It was a quick and tidy process. While they waited for a unit to arrive to take David Benson to a local precinct, he'd said nothing. Even when Tess and Jake had asked him direct questions, Benson remained silent, with a stern look of anger on his face. At first glance, the reaction was yet another nail in his coffin—another indicator that he was their killer.

But something about it felt a little off to Tessa. There was a piece to it all—to his demeanor and the entire situation—that didn't seem to fit. It nagged at her even now, as they watched the patrol car with David Benson in the back drive away from the construction site. In the silence that followed with just her and Jake among the shadows of buildings yet to come, it continued to eat at her.

"You know," Jake said. "During that chase, I saw quite a bit of the tenacity that helped you destroy all those course records."

"And in the dark, at that," she said, trying to inject some humor into it.

"Hey, Tessa? Let me see your arm."

She almost argued but knew better. Besides, she knew her injuries needed some attention. She extended her arm to him, and he frowned right away. He used the flashlight on his phone to have a look, pulling aside the bandages from earlier in the day.

"That's already starting to bruise," he said. "Can you twist your arm at all?"

She did, and there was no pain. She knew what he was looking for, though. Even though she couldn't register the pain, her very body would understand when something was broken or out of order. If her arm had been broken, it wouldn't be able to twist or properly support a fully functioning hand. The blow had caused a bruise that was already darkening up like ripe fruit, but nothing was broken.

"You still haven't cleaned these cuts?" he asked.

"No."

He frowned at her, but he'd learned long ago in their partnership not to push matters like this. She knew the dangers involved. With her CIPA-like condition, any cut or abrasion could be lethal. If it got infected or was too deep and her pain receptors were unable to decipher the threat level, it could lead to infection. And infection could lead to sickness. If she were a typical CIPA patient, that sickness would lead to death. But she was, as some of the doctors had said, a unicorn. That last grisly part wasn't part of her condition. When others got sick, she seemed to thrive. No one had made sense of it despite the barrage of doctor's visits and medical tests.

"Will you do me a favor?" he asked. "As your partner…and as your friend?"

"What's that?"

"When we leave here, we'll lead back to Benson's house and have a look around. See what we can find. And then we'll head down to the precinct and question him. But before we get into that interrogation room, I want you to find a first aid kit and a bathroom, and I want you to properly clean these."

"Yeah, I can do that."

Their eyes locked in the darkness, and for a fleeting moment, the world seemed to hold its breath. There was something there, in the space between them, a recognition of strength and mutual respect that shimmered like heat on pavement. She'd felt it before in similar moments but had thought nothing of it. Just the thrill of the chase, adrenaline having its way. But it was more than that now—it was the burgeoning spark of something neither had anticipated.

"Let's just hope he's our guy," Tessa spoke into the silence, breaking the spell as she turned back to the construction site.

"Well, let's go see what else we can find," Jake said.

They walked through the night together, heading back to Benson's house and wondering what other morbid pieces they might find to the puzzle.

CHAPTER TWELVE

The busy rumblings of the law enforcement headquarters engulfed Tessa as she and Jake made their way through a labyrinth of desks and murmurs. David Benson was currently in an interrogation room and from what they were being told, he still hadn't' spoken a single word since spitting in Tessa's face. He hadn't even asked for a lawyer.

Tessa thought his reaction might change when he saw what they'd found in his house. They hadn't found much to help convict him, but what they *did* find was pretty damning. There was a notebook, found in his small office, that listed the crime scenes and details of each of the pearl necklace murders. They were items in a very long list of crimes that had occurred in Portland and surrounding areas over the past years, all scrawled down in his small, tight handwriting.

The notebook was currently in Jake's hand, sealed up in an evidence bag.

They reached the interrogation room, a copy of so many other interrogation rooms Tessa had spent time in—a featureless, soundproof square designed to isolate and intimidate. A one-way mirror to the right reflected their grim procession. Tessa wondered how many were on the other side watching. With three bodies to account for so far, she wondered if Special Agent Charge Rebecca Lawson would end up down here to listen in.

Benson looked up at them with uncertainty in his eyes. At some point, someone had brought him a bottle of water. His right hand was cuffed to one of the legs of the standard metal table near the center of the room. He was sitting up rigidly as if glued to the chair. She saw some of his defiance still lingering in his face but, as was the case with most criminals, things seemed to have softened a bit ever since landing in an interrogation room.

His gaze darted between Tessa and Jake, and then to the mirror, where he knew unseen eyes scrutinized his every move. The corners of his mouth twitched, and for a moment, irritation flared in his eyes.

Jake tossed the newly discovered notebook down on the table. The slap of it was like a tiny bomb in the room.

“We found this at your house,” Jake said. “In your office. And it’s making things look so much worse for you. So if I were you, I’d start talking *now.”*

Benson looked down at the table, his free hand nervously clutching the water bottle. "I don't know what you want me to say."

“Well, let me start,” Tessa said. “Let me tell you the puzzle we’re looking at—a puzzle that includes a pearl, your fingerprint, and three dead women. Edith Harper was killed tonight, murdered in the same fashion two other women within the past four days: Mary Rogers and Regina Flowers, both strangled with pearl necklaces. And a trip to the FBI labs quickly provided a print on a loose pearl we found at Ms. Harper’s home.”

“That,” Jake said, “with the details you’ve lined out in this notebook add up to a pretty nasty picture, Mr. Benson.”

Benson tilted his head and, though he still looked a bit uncertain, he said: “You think I killed a woman? *Three* women?”

“That’s where things are pointing right now, yes,” Tessa said. “Oh, and your having a peek at a *very* recently murdered woman on Facebook doesn’t help, either. Especially not when your fingerprints were found on an item in her home on the same night.”

She observed him closely, her senses heightened by the gravity of the situation. His confidence seemed to waver, like a flickering light bulb unsure of its power. There was something in the way his eye twitched when they pressed him, a hint of something genuine behind his performance.

"Tell me about Edith Harper," Tessa said softly, intentionally steering away from direct accusations. "Why her?"

“Listen…” Benson said. He nodded to the notebook in its evidence bag and said, “Edith Harper is the last entry in that book, right?”

“She is,” Jake conceded.

“And how many entries do you think are in there?”

“We’re the ones asking the questions, Mr. Benson,” Tessa snapped.

“Fine. I can tell you that there are at least eighty entries in there. Surely you don’t think I’m responsible for all of them.”

“We’re not insinuating that,” Tessa said. “The better question is *why* you have these entries at all.”

David's face was a canvas of conflicting emotions as he struggled to maintain his veneer of indifference. His lips parted, then closed, as if the words were fighting to stay within.

"Because it's interesting. Crimes scenes, murder, police procedurals.”

“I don’t understand,” Jake said.

David sighed, almost as if he were embarrassed of what came next. “There’s a police band radio app on my phone. I used to have an actual police band radio, but it was out of date and wasn't very reliable. I spend a lot of time listening in. And if I catch wind of a really bad crime, I do a deep dive when I can. I heard about Ms. Harper and started researching.”

"An interesting hobby," Tessa commented, her mind churning through the implications. "Why the fascination?"

"Understanding," he replied in a whisper, almost to himself. “Understanding darkness.”

Tessa's eyes narrowed, analyzing his demeanor. He was an enigma, a man whose psyche seemed to be a patchwork of contradictions. Was he a cold-blooded killer or just a troubled soul with a macabre interest? It was hard to tell, as his mood seemed to be switching back and forth.

“So to study Ms. Harper in more detail, you went to her Facebook page?” Jack asked.

“Yeah. And other things. News articles about her, things like that.””

“Did you know her?” Tessa asked.

"Not well. I knew who she was. She was a teacher for a long time. Retired last year, from what I understand."

“And how do you know that?”

"Kids on my street had her as a teacher. A few of them…maybe as many as three or four. Not my neighbor, but the house down from *that*. I'm friends with them, and they have a daughter who had Ms. Harper during her final year…last year."

Tessa didn't like where this was going. She could feel him slipping away despite the two glaring bits of evidence: the fingerprint and the fact that he'd run from them.

“Why’d you run from us then?” Tessa asked. “If all you were doing was snooping around, trying to find more information about a recent murder from home, why run?”

“I was scared. The FBI came knocking at eleven o’ clock at night and I was eavesdropping on police chatter about a woman’s murder. I freaked out.”

“I say bullshit,” Jake said. “Your fingerprint was on that pearl. How do you explain that?”

Benson shook his head. “I don’t…that, I don’t know.”

“It’s not difficult,” Jake said. “At some point today, a string of pearls passed through your hands. And one of those pearls was found at the scene of a murder. Mr. Benson, surely you understand what this looks like, right?"

With a sudden surge of motion, Benson threw the water bottle across the room. It bounced from the wall, the top still on and spilling nothing. The sudden violence made Tessa flinch inwardly, but outwardly she remained stoic, unperturbed.

"I'm no killer! I just…I like the idea of crime scenes. I like thinking about those dead people…the way they had no idea it was their last day. The way…"

He started shaking his head slowly back and forth. Tessa and Jake shared an uncomfortable glance. Tessa *really* didn't like the way this was going. She'd seen several suspects try to play this act before…to make it seem as if they were unhinged in an attempt to squirm out of whatever charges had been brought against them.

But she didn't think this was an act. She thought David Benson may be a bit mentally unsound. Slowly, she approached the table and sat down at one of the free chairs. She kept her voice soft and measured when she spoke.

"David…I need you to be honest with me. Did you kill Edith Harper?"

Still shaking his head, he said, "No."

"How about Mary Rogers and Regina Flowers? Their names are in your notebook, too."

"No. I knew they…knew they were dead. I listened to the radio. I even drove by their homes the day after. But no…I'm not…*I'm not the killer!"*

Yeah, I really don't think you are, she thought.

She looked at Jack and nodded her head toward the door. He started in that direction, and as he opened the door, Tessa glanced back at David Benson. "Give us a moment, Mr. Benson."

They stepped out into the hallway, and Tessa closed the door behind her. In the relative quiet of the hallway, Jake said, "What do you think?"

"I think we need to pull medical records for him. I think he may be mentally unsound. And I don't…Jesus, Jake. I don't think it's him. But that fingerprint on the pearl is hard to ignore. That's a smoking gun."

"Here's what we'll do," Jake said. "I'll go see if I can pull medical records…see if there's anything there. Maybe you can get alibis out of him. See if he's even come into contact with pearls in the last few days."

Tessa knew it was the next logical step, but she already feared it might be a waste of time. She nodded and, without another word, walked back into the interrogation room. A quick, flickering image of Sarah's face appeared in her mind, but she managed to swat it away.

Tessa returned to her chair, the ghost of a sigh escaping her. Her experience told her that killers could be convincing liars, but intuition whispered that David Benson was many things, none of them good, but not a murderer. Not this time.

"Thank you for your continued cooperation, Mr. Benson," she said, the formality returning to her voice as she stood up, signaling the end of the interrogation. "I wonder if you might be able to tell me where you've been the last few nights."

“At home. I don’t get out much.”

“And what do you do for work?”

“A delivery driver for Newman Brands.”

“That’s the snack cake and chip company, right?”

“Right.”

She noticed that he had come down from whatever manic fit had taken him while he’d been shaking his head. “So…you have no alibis?”

“Probably not. Not after like eight or so, anyway. My neighbors see me most afternoons while I’m coming in from work.”

“Maybe your internet browser can back your time at home up? Maybe shows you streamed, things like that?”

He shrugged as if he really didn’t care. “I don’t know. You can check whatever…whatever you want.”

"David," she said softly, breaking the silence that had settled between them like dust. "I need you to talk to me about your past."

He scoffed a derisive sound that bounced off the walls. "What's there to say? It's messed up, like everyone else's."

"David, so you see any specialists? Maybe for your physical or mental health?”

He smirked and chuckled. "Oh, yeah. A shrink. Been seeing shrinks for years. I may be bipolar. Another word they toss around is cyclothymia. Sounds fancy, right?"

His facade crumbled suddenly, as if her words were the final blow to a dam holding back a flood. His shoulders shook, and he buried his face in his hands, his breath coming in gasps that echoed in the small room.

"Nobody understands," he choked out, tears seeping through his fingers. "The voices, they don't stop. They're always there, whispering... I can't make them go away."

Tessa felt a twinge of sympathy, her heart clenching at the sight of this broken man. She knew all too well how the demons of the mind could torment a soul without respite. And while she knew a mental condition like this did not in any way immediately eliminate him as a suspect, she was all but convinced he was not the killer.

"David, have these problems led you to hurt anyone?" she inquired, her tone careful not to push him over an edge he seemed perilously close to.

"Never," he sobbed. "I could never hurt another person. I know what pain feels like."

Observing him, Tessa's instincts whispered that his anguish was genuine. A criminal, perhaps, but not a cold-blooded killer. His misery spoke of torment, not malice.

"Thank you for being honest with us," she managed to say, though her voice betrayed her disappointment.

David's only response was a muted nod, his eyes still downcast, lost in a world of inner turmoil.

Exiting the room, Tessa caught her reflection in the one-way mirror—her expression was one of a woman who carried the weight of unsolved tragedies. She paused for a moment, allowing herself to feel the gravity of their predicament. The ticking of the precinct clock drilled into her consciousness, reminding her of the precious time slipping away with each second.

They couldn't let David go. The fingerprint on the pearl was just too damning. But based on the interrogation with him, Tessa hurried along the hall to find Jake, certain that this case was far from over. She needed to keep making links to find more pieces to the puzzle. She knew that Edith Harper was single—a widow, in fact—but maybe she had more family in town. And if so, they were the next stop, hopefully able to give them a clearer picture of this new, tragic piece to the puzzle.

CHAPTER THIRTEEN

Tessa felt a slight sting of guilt when she saw that there was already a patrol car parked in front of the residence of Michael Harper. This meant someone else had already suffered the misfortune of breaking the news. Tessa considered herself tough-natured, but telling someone that a loved one had died was among the hardest part of her job—and she'd done it far too often.

"Here we go," Jake said, reaching for the door handle and stepping out into the summer night. It was slightly muggy and the air felt thick with apprehension, but it was a beautiful night, otherwise.

But Michael Harper probably doesn't think so, Tessa thought.

Tessa and Jake approached the door, which swung open before they could knock, revealing a uniformed female cop. She was on the younger side, maybe only a year or two older than Tessa's twenty-four years. Tessa and Jake showed their credentials, and the officer gestured for them to come in.

"Is it just you who's here?" Tessa asked the officer.

"No. My partner is in the kitchen with Mr. Harper. He's...well, he's in quite a state of shock but has been holding it together quite well for the past five minutes or so."

"That's understandable," Tessa said as she and Jake walked further into the house.

The house was a bit of a mess, but an organized one—the sort of mess most people might ignore completely and describe the house as "lived in." Tessa noted the two backpacks by the front door, small shoes tucked neatly under a small hallway table. As they walked down the hallway and towards the shining surfaces of the kitchen, she saw pictures of a man she assumed to be Michael Harper with a gorgeous, redheaded wife and two adorable daughters. The oldest looked to be ten or so if the framed pictures were recent.

As they entered the kitchen, the other cop looked relieved to see them. He was considerably molder than the woman at the door, his thick gray moustache highlighting the difference. Tessa again showed their credentials, and the cop nodded. He stepped to the side of the room, angling between the kitchen table and a column-shaped window that looked out to the side yard.

Michael Harper was sitting at the kitchen bar, propped on a stool. He was slouched and resting his arms on the counter, looking like he might fall off at any moment. His eyes were red-rimmed and weary. In the den behind him, his wife was speaking quietly to someone on the phone, her face a mask of sadness.

"FBI agents, right?," Michael asked, his voice strained but polite.

"Yes," Tessa said. "Mr. Harper, we're very sorry for your loss, and the last thing I want to seem is uncaring or rude, but we—

"Need to ask questions. I know. Officer King here already told me you'd be coming and that it was pressing. He said…said there had been others who had been killed the same way?"

"Yes. Two others. The exact same way. So we believe we're dealing with a serial killer that isn't showing any signs of slowing down. So any help you could provide…"

"If I can, I'd be glad to," he said, though his voice squeaked a bit. Tessa didn't think he was going to be able to hold it together much longer.

"Michael," she began, her voice low and even, "I'd like to start by trying to piece together your mother's life—her habits, her friends. Hopefully, we can come up with links between her and the others, and it will point us to our guilty party."

"Sure, that sounds smart."

"First of all, can you think of any changes in her life recently? Anything unusual?"

"She...she was a creature of habit. Up at dawn every day with a. cup of coffee out on her patio. She retired last year after thirty-five years with the same school, so that's been different. She was always griping about how she had nothing to do. She got bored easily. That's why she spent so much time tending to her garden, I suppose."

"Her garden?"

"Yes." Michael's eyes lit up for a moment, a brief respite from his grief. "Mom had an affinity for English roses. She'd spend hours with them. Even talked to them, I think."

Tessa could almost picture Ms. Harper among her blooms, a serene figure lost in the simple joy of nurturing life. But the image was marred by the shadow of the investigation—the presence of a 'creepy worker' to use Regina Flowers' terminology. Had someone fitting that description been part of her life as well?

"Was there anyone new in her life?" Tessa asked. "Someone out of the ordinary who might have shared this interest in gardening?"

"Actually, there was a gardener..." Michael hesitated, then shook his head. "But he was just a hired hand. Came recommended."

"Tell us about the gardener," Jake prompted, peering closely at a nearby trellis.

"His name is George. Seemed like a decent guy, kept to himself mostly. Mom trusted him, let him bring over some rare species to plant here."

"George," Tessa repeated, the name registering in her mental ledger. "We'll need to speak with him."

"Yeah, sure. I actually think I have his card around here somewhere. Katherine—that's my wife—was really taken by Mom's roses and thought she might try her hand at it. I can grab it for you if you need it."

Before Tessa could respond, a soft and raspy voice spoke up from the den. "I'll get it," Katherine said, now off of the phone. Her eyes and face were streaked with tears, and Tessa could see the heartbreak for her husband in the drooping of her lips.

"Thanks, sweetie," Michael said, basically on autopilot. Tessa really didn't think he'd last much longer before he allowed himself to break.

"Mr. Harper, I have what might seem like a strange question, but I assure you that it's pertinent to the case. Do you know if your mother had any pearl jewelry?"

Michael blinked, surprised. He looked almost spooked, in fact. as if pulled from a reverie. "Yes, actually. She always wore these pearl earrings. Had them since she was a teenager, said they were a gift from her own mother. She wore them every day without fail."

Pearl earrings. A detail that could be innocuous or everything. Tessa filed it away, knowing full well the significance of pearls in this twisted case. She made a mental note to revisit the forensic reports. Those earrings could speak volumes. Though, as she thought back to the crime scene, she was quite certain Ms. Edith Harper had not been wearing pearl earrings.

"Every day, you say?" Tessa prompted, watching Michael closely.

"Every single day." He touched his earlobe unconsciously, a gesture of memory. "Even when gardening."

"Speaking of routines," Tessa continued, her voice steady despite the churn of her thoughts. "Were there any services or workers other than George, the gardener? Anyone who would have had direct access to your mother's home?"

Michael hesitated, a flicker of uncertainty in his eyes. “I don’t think so. Just George.”

"Another odd question for you, and we'll leave you alone for now. Do you know if your mother frequented a pool?"

“I’m ashamed to say I’m not sure. I know she *talked* about joining a water aerobic class at the YMCA, but I don’t know if she ever did.”

His face pinched up at this, and a trail of tears erupted from his eyes—likely because he realized there was so much he hadn't known about his mother even though she lived just fifteen minutes away. And now she was gone.

"Thank you, Michael," Tessa said finally. "You've been very helpful."

He nodded, but buried his head in his arms, beginning to let out a series of hitching sobs. As Tessa and Jake turned away to head back down the hall, Katherine approached them. She’d started crying again at the sound of her husband’s sorrow.

“Here,” she said, handing them the business card for George, the gardener. “And please…do whatever you can to catch the monster who did this.”

She then hurried away from them, rushing to be by her husband’s side. Tessa glanced at the pictures on the wall again, wondering if the two little girls were sleeping soundly upstairs. She imagined them waking up in the morning to find that they no longer had a grandmother.

It infuriated her. It itched at her like a poison under her skin, escorting her out of the home of Michael Harper. They were halfway to her car when the shrill ring of her cell phone sliced through the early morning hours.

She answered it on the second ring. "Flint here."

Rebecca Lawson's voice was calm yet stern on the other end. "Flint, I need you and Sullivan at H.Q. right now. We've had a development in your case."

“What is it?” Tessa asked, already rushing to the car and urging Jake along.

"We've got a message from your killer. And Tessa," she paused, a rare tremor in her hardened tone, "it's not good."

CHAPTER FOURTEEN

"Okay, what do we have?" Tessa asked, her eyes scanning the room, absorbing every detail. She caught snippets of conversation about decryption efforts and behavioral analyses, but her focus remained fixed on the crux of the moment—the taunting letter.

A tangible electricity hung in the air of the Portland field office, buzzing through the halls and rooms of the building. It was made worse by the fact that the usual placid atmosphere was currently gone, replaced by a crescendo of frenzied energy. Agents swarming like bees disturbed from their hive, frenzied over this letter sent by a killer who now seemed to not be just interested in murder, but attention.

"See for yourself," Lawson said. Sliding a large envelope over to her. It was in a clear evidence bag, giving it an almost dangerous, foreboding feeling.

As Tessa picked up the bag and looked at the letter for the first time, the air itself felt heavy with consequence. She poured over the handwriting that seemed to dance with a perverse kind of glee as Jake stepped in beside her.

"This looks like random ranting," Jake said.

"It does," Tessa agreed. "But I'm sure it's not."

She took a moment to read it out loud, allowing her tongue to feel each word, for her mind to absorb each syllable and to look for hidden meanings.

The moon itself is a pearl, and all will wilt beneath its light. Strangled by beauty, in death, they lose their luster. Crowds of the elegant dead staring blindly at the PEARLY gates."

"The moon," Jake said. "He's killed all three at night. That could be something. Maybe he's telling us he's going to stick to his routine."

"Let's not get lost in the poetry of it." Tessa's voice was firm, commanding attention. "This killer enjoys the game, the attention. We need to step back, look at the bigger picture. And there *is* a big picture. He's put the word 'pearly' in all caps for a reason."

"And in reference to the pearly gates," one of the analysts at the end of the table said.

"Well, he's clearly obsessed with pearls," Tessa said. "He sees them as heavenly, but he's also using them to kill women. They're symbolic to him. Like heaven is for some."

"Or maybe he's trying to be double-clever," Jake said. "Maybe he thinks he's doing them a favor by killing them and sending them to those pearly gates."

"Could be," one of the other analysts said. Tessa notes that this analyst, a young and intense-looking woman of about twenty-five, was staring at a copy of the letter, copying the words with her own pen, working on handwriting analysis. Tessa hated to think such a thing while everyone was obviously working very hard, but she thought it might be a massive waste of time.

"There's something else I think we should consider," Tessa said.

"What's that?" Lawson asked.

"That he only sent this to rub our nose in his success. The letter could mean absolutely nothing—just a surefire way to get us working harder, maybe to pull us off into another trail. The entire thing could be nothing but bullshit."

"I agree," Lawson said. "But, Agent Flint…you know that's a very dangerous assumption."

"Each pearl has been moderately different so far," Tessa said. "if there are answers to be had—clear answers, that's where we'll find them."

She took out her phone and snapped pictures of the letter. The room remained mostly quiet as she did so, as there was now a new tension in the air; she could feel everyone's eyes on her, wondering if she was going to join the effort to decrypt and further analyze the letter or if she was going to venture off on her own again, firmly believing the letter to be useless.

She did feel that they were wasting time and manpower on this letter. Yes, it was an important development in the case, but somewhere out there, a killer waited, and an innocent life hung in the balance. With each passing second, the weight of this knowledge bore down upon her shoulders, heavy and unyielding.

"With your permission," Tessa said, looking directly at SAIC Lawson, "I'd like to delve further into these pearls. There's something we're missing."

"Like what?"

"I'd like to speak with a gemologist. Someone who would know everything there is to know about a pearl."

“I understand you’ve been working with Dr. Carter Lucas at the lab,” Lawson said. “Can’t he help?”

"He's brilliant, yes—but I need someone with a laser-sharp focus on pearls and gems. So we have anyone like that in our network?”

“If we do, Dr. Carter is going to be able to get it for you faster than I could. But why are you so certain that’s where we’ll find the answers you need to close this case?”

"Given the quality of these pearls, they're not common purchases. Our killer might be leaving us pieces of his own story," Tessa said while typing out a message with focused intensity. "Let's not forget how he leaves the pearls—carefully arranged, intentional. It's theatrical—like this letter. He wants us to know that these aren’t random acts of violence. There's a narrative here. And the pearls are key to understanding it."

"Then we need to uncover what they mean to him," Jake said. "If the pearls are his signature, there’s got to be a story behind them."

"Which is why we need an expert," Tessa concluded, her gaze locking onto Jake's. “Someone who can give us insight into their significance beyond their monetary value.”

“And what about the suspect you currently still have in custody—a Mr. David Benson?”

“The fingerprint on the pearl found at the scene of Edith Harper’s murder is inescapable. But there are so many other bits of evidence and even his alibis that—”

“Yes, I read that report. But you understand that if you can’t find anyone else and we find another victim, that’s a risky certainty on your part.”

“It is. But with all due respect, if someone else is murdered while Benson is in custody, that also proves he’s not the killer.”

Tessa was aware that there was an audience of nine others listening to this back and forth and worried that it may be flirting with disrespect. She nodded to Lawson and said, “So, if it’s okay with you, I’ll call Dr. Carter and see if he can come up with a gemologist contact.”

“Yes, that’s fine.”

Tessa gave the entire room a cursory nod as she and Jake headed back out into the hall, just over five minutes after reporting into the conference room.

“You really think the letter is useless?” Jake asked quietly as they made their way to the stairs.

“Not completely useless, no. That’s why I took some pictures of it. But I don’t think it’s nearly as important as the pearls themselves. That letter is a distraction more than anything else.”

What she didn’t say out loud was that there was indeed something eerie about the letter. *Strangled by beauty, in death, they lose their luster. Crowds of the elegant dead staring blindly at the PEARLY gates.*

As she and Jake started up the stairs, Tessa pulled out her phone. She scrolled through her contacts, searching for Lucas's number. She thought he might very well be able to connect them with an expert…and she also hoped he might have a read on the pearl from Edith Harper’s house.

"Lucas will know someone," Tessa said, more to herself than to Jake, as she made the call. "A gemologist could help us decipher the language of those pearls, maybe even the psyche behind them."

"Let's hope so," Jake replied, as they stepped outside and he glanced over his shoulder at the imposing structure they'd just left behind. "Because right now, that's the best lead we have."

The phone rang three times before it was picked up. "Hey there, gent Flint," Dr. Lucas Carter said in the way of a greeting. "Sorry to disappoint you, but I don't have anything solid on that pearl just yet."

“That’s perfectly fine,” she said. “I’m actually calling for something else. We need your help finding a gemologist. Someone that would know about pearls on an almost intimate level."

“That’s…uh, well, that’s a tough one. I think I can send you a name or two, but you'll have to give me a few minutes."

“That’s fine,” she said. “Just call me as soon as you get it.”

She ended the call as they reached the car. She looked out into the dark night, the parking lot illuminated by the sparse streetlights installed along its length. Peering into the darkness, she couldn’t keep her mind from wondering what their killer was doing right then, at that very moment.

Was he planning his next attack, or was he already in the midst of it?

CHAPTER FIFTEEN

The room was mundane in its simplicity, the walls barren save for peeling beige paint. It could have been anyone's living room in any small town, but this nondescript space was a sanctuary of sinister intent. A single bulb dangled from a frayed cord above, casting feeble light upon the hall table, which served as a macabre altar. The surface was cluttered with an array of photographs, the smiles forever frozen in time—faces that would never smile again. Each image was a trophy, each face a conquest.

His gaze panned over not just the pictures but the collection of mementos he'd taken: a watch, a pair of earrings, a hair ribbon. But it was the pearls that called to him—two strands of them lying amidst the chaos like a serpent poised to strike.

He reached out, fingers trembling with anticipation, and lifted the pearls that had once belonged to Regina Flowers. They were cool to the touch, each orb smooth and lustrous, a stark contrast to the warmth of life they had once encircled. He closed his eyes, allowing the memory to wash over him—the power, the control. The last breath quivered through her lips as the world fell away from her terrified eyes.

In the stillness, he could almost hear the echo of her pleading, the futile struggle against the inevitable. He could almost feel the tension in her muscles as she fought against him, the way her body thrashed beneath his unyielding grip. The struggle was brief—a fleeting dance of desperation. His lips curled into a grim smile at the recollection of how the necklace had tightened, bead by bead, until stillness had overcome her.

He cherished these moments, the intimacy of the kill; it was an art form, and he, a connoisseur of death.

More than that, he was *good* at it and oh God, he'd started to enjoy it. He'd started to enjoy it so much that he also relished the idea that there were now people after him—cops, the FBI, and probably a number of others as well. He was so confident in himself and so intoxicated by the thrill of it all that he'd sent a letter to the FBI's local field office. He figured if he continued to kill unabated and without capture, he may even send one to D.C.

He placed the pearls back onto the table with reverence, his thoughts already turning towards the next dance, the next display of his mastery over life and death. The hunger within him grew, a gnawing need for another soul to add to his collection. He had a list…a rather long list that he was starting to think he may actually be able to get through.

And when it was exhausted, maybe he'd move elsewhere and start again.

The killer's fingers, pale and delicate as the pearls they caressed, worked meticulously with a small, damp cloth. Each circular motion on the smooth surface was methodical, a silent tribute to the precision with which he executed each step of his plans.

As he laid down the cleansed strand of pearls, his eyes caught sight of the second string, one untouched by human warmth, lying solitary upon the table. It gleamed under the dull light, an unfulfilled promise waiting patiently for its destined throat. He reached out, allowing his fingertips to hover above it, not touching—yet.

The anticipation of selecting who would wear this set sent a thrill through him, a dark pleasure that stirred him deeply. This new string of pearls, unmarked by history, was a blank canvas awaiting his artistry, an opportunity to craft another masterpiece in his expanding gallery of silenced lives.

"Patience," he told himself, his voice like that of a phantom in his lair. The game was afoot, and he was both the player and the game master. There was no rush—the hunt was part of the joy, the savoring of each moment leading up to the inevitable conclusion. Each pearl seemed to understand its role in his grand design, its luster a mute accomplice to the sinister fate it would soon bestow.

From within the depths of his mind, faces swirled like specters at a masquerade—all chosen for their elegance, for their comfortable position at the top of society where they could look down on the lesser people below. Lesser people like him.

His thoughts drifted to the list he'd put together—stowed away in his mind but never written own. Writing it down seemed too foolish, too dangerous. But he'd seen them all and had even conversed with a few of them—women who walked the edge of his periphery, not knowing they had been marked for death.

Unable to sit still any longer, he got to his feet. Sure, he'd taken the life of Edith Harper less than eight hours ago, but his hands were already desperate to get to work again. He knew he must be patient, but…it was far too hard at times.

With purposeful strides, he approached the door, the string of pearls now secure in his jacket pocket, their future etched in the dark recesses of his intent. As he reached for the doorknob, he glanced back at his lair, the tableau of his twisted achievements bearing silent testimony to the past.

And there was so much more room left on that table to fill.

CHAPTER SIXTEEN

During her four years as an agent, Tessa had only come to the mineralogy lab three times before the pearl necklace killer case. But at just after two o'clock in the morning –just an hour after asking Lucas for a gemology contact, she found herself arriving in the dimly lit labs for the third time in just as many days. It had become an unexpected epicenter in her search for a murderer.

And now it was also going to be the location of a Zoom call with the gemologist Lucas had found for them. Being that the expert lived in Pasadena, California, this ate-night call made the most sense in terms of time and the case.

Lucas was still there, now just as deeply involved in the case as Tessa or Jake. She and Jake found him hunched over his microscope, peering intently at the pearl from Edith Harper's residence. He looked up as they entered, and Tessa instantly noted the sour expression on his face.

"Nothing new?" she asked.

"Nothing yet. This one looks like your basic, run-of-the-mill pearl. Does that…well, does that mean anything to you?"

"Sadly, no. We don't even know what the hell we're looking for."

"Thanks for setting this call up, though," Jake said. "It saved us a lot of time and hassle."

"Of course. I've already got you guys set up on a laptop in the office all the way to the back. Dr. Harrison is waiting for your call." He pointed to the back wall of the room, a door standing open to reveal a well-lit office beyond.

"Well, let's not keep the man waiting," Jake chimed in, rolling up his sleeves as he settled beside Tessa in front of the computer screen.

Lucas had already set the Zoom interface up, so all Tessa had to do was join the call. They went through right away, and Tessa found herself looking at the bespectacled face of a man who looked roughly fifty or so.

"Hello," the man—presumably the Dr. Harrison that Lucas had mentioned—said. "You're Agents Flint and Sullivan, I take it?"

"We are," Tessa said. "And you are…?"

“Dr. Ben Harrison. Dr. Carter and I have worked in tandem on a few off cases, so it’s always exciting to get his call…even at such a late hour. Now…he says you’ve got a head-scratcher of a case on your hands. Something to do with pearls?

"That's right. We have reason to believe that pearls are a significant aspect of a case we're working on," Tessa explained succinctly. She then spent roughly two minutes filling him in on the details of the case. Harrison nodded along and took copious notes, scribbling them down just off-screen.

“Okay, that sounds pretty awful,” he said when Tessa was done. “So, what do you need from me?"

“A few things,” Tessa said. "For starters, could you enlighten us on the different types of pearls and their formation processes? Any cultural symbolism attached to them may be crucial, too."

"Of course." Dr. Harrison adjusted his glasses as if to bring the full weight of his expertise into focus. "Pearls can broadly be classified as natural or cultured. Natural pearls are formed when an irritant, often a parasite, works its way into an oyster. As a defense mechanism, the mollusk secretes layers of nacre around it."

Tessa visualized the process, likening it to how she encapsulated her own emotions during a case—layer by layer until a semblance of normalcy was restored.

"Whereas cultured pearls," Dr. Harrison continued, "are creations of human intervention. A technician inserts a piece of mantle tissue into the mollusk to kickstart the process. There's artistry involved, a very precise and underappreciated form. Each pearl is unique, reflecting the conditions of its creation."

"Interesting," Jake muttered, scribbling notes of his own on a pad Lucas had provided. "And the symbolism?"

"Ah, pearls have long been associated with purity and wisdom across various cultures. But they also represent transformation—quite fitting, given their origin from a simple grain of sand to an object of beauty."

Tessa felt the weight of Dr. Harrison's words settle upon her, stirring a new perspective within the labyrinth of her thoughts. Every victim, every clue—they were grains of sand being coated with layers of truth, slowly forming the pearl that was the solution to this enigmatic case.

“Can you think of anything in history that might somehow link pearls or even just their cultivation with ritualistic murder or sacrifices?”

“No. And believe it or not, it’s a question I’ve been asked multiple times during my career. But in all of my extensive research, I’ve never seen it pop up all. The closest you’ll find has to do with pirates on the sea, taking out entire platoons of people for gold and jewelry—much of which was pearl-based—but that’s about it.”

Tessa sighed; she felt that the conversation was already over. She’d learned quite a bit but wasn’t sure how any of the new information could be tied to the case.

“I can see by the look on your face that you were hoping for something more,” Harrison said.

“Truthfully, yes,” Tessa said. “But we do greatly appreciate your time. Thanks so much, Dr. Harrison.”

“Of course. Good luck you, and let me know if I can help in any other way.”

He gave a polite nod to the screen and as the call ended and the window shrank away on the screen, Tessa sat back, her mind racing. Her gaze fell upon the array of mineral samples lined neatly on the shelves behind the office desk, each one a silent witness to the relentless march of time and transformation. She considered the pearls—their secrets now partially unveiled—and felt the thrill of the chase pulse through her veins.

She turned to Jake, who was tapping a pen against the notepad, a rhythmic staccato that seemed to echo the ticking of her brain as it worked to decode the significance of what they'd just learned.

"Dr. Harrison mentioned that cultured pearls can be... manipulated," Tessa began, her voice carrying the weight of revelation. "Each one is unique, made so by human intervention. It’s like the killer sees his victims as canvases for his sick artistry."

Jake nodded slowly, his eyes dark with understanding. "Maybe the injection is part of that. He injects them, and they go limp…numb. This way, maybe he's sort of letting their reactions form the pearl—or the *artwork*. And he leaves them for us, a display of his control over the transformation."

"It’s as good a theory as any," Tessa agreed, feeling the pieces click into place. "A warped admiration for his victims, an obsession with creating beauty from pain." Her hands clenched at her sides, the frustration of not being able to stop this twisted individual coursing through her like an electric current.

"Each victim has been chosen for a reason, each one represents something to him," Jake said thoughtfully. "If we can decipher that meaning, we might be able to predict his next move."

“And again, maybe it’s simpler than all that,” Tessa offered. “Maybe he’s just going after rich women. Maybe he hates upper-class royalty.”

“Whatever it is,” Jake said, “we better stop the bastard.”

“And without any sustainable leads, that’s getting harder and harder to do.”

As the lab's overhead lights hummed quietly above them, Tessa felt the chase narrowing, the gap closing between them and the enigmatic figure lurking always two steps ahead in the shadows.

"I say we head back to the office,” she said. “We can gather everything we know about the victims and work on that angle rather than trying to make sense of the killer. We need to find the thread that ties them together, the reason he chose them…and see if there’s anything there that goes beyond wealth and status."

They got up from the table and, after giving a wave of thanks to Lucas, headed back upstairs to the main floor. Tessa felt that she was getting to know this building a little too well.

"His obsession with pearls—it's more than a signature," she said as they neared the doors. The night waited, heavy and black on the other side. "It's a message. Each pearl is a chapter in his story. But what is it he's trying to tell us?"

It was a rhetorical question, so she wasn’t upset when Jake didn’t have an answer to offer. They made their way back to the car in silence, everything still and quiet in the night around them. Tessa felt her boy demanding some sleep, but she knew there was no time for that. If she had her way, she'd not sleep another wink until they'd captured their killer.

When they were in the car, Jake behind the wheel and starting the engine, he finally broke the daunting silence. "You okay?"

"I’m fine," she muttered, not meeting his eyes. "Just trying to piece everything together."

"Listen," he said. "We're making progress. We have a better understanding of the killer's MO now than we did before. And we'll keep digging until we find what we need to catch him.”

“Yeah…”

“How long have we been partners?” he asked, a smile forming at the corners of his mouth.

“A little over two years.”

“And we’ve worked…what? Maybe twenty-five cases together?”

"Something like that." She knew where he was going with this, but let him finish. Sometimes, it was nice to her encouragement…even when it did little to lift the spirits.

"And how many have we *not* closed?"

"Just one."

"Damned good odds if you ask me. We *are* going to get this guy, Tessa."

Despite his words, Tessa couldn't shake off the sense of discouragement that weighed heavily on her. She felt like they were running out of time, that every second wasted was another opportunity for the killer to strike.

"Can I ask you something?" Jake said, his tone gentle. He'd not yet pulled out of the parking space, the car idling in the parking lot of the lab.

"Sure."

"Your condition," he said, referring to her inability to feel pain. "How has it shaped your life?"

Tessa hesitated for a moment, considering her answer. It wasn't a topic she liked to dwell on, but she trusted Jake enough to share with him. And she didn't see what it had to do with the case. Still, it was rare for Jake to broach the topic with such bluntness. He knew all about it, and they'd discussed it a few times before. Surely, there was a reason.

"You *know* that's a loaded question."

"Oh, I know," he said with a smile. "And I know how you squirm whenever I ask you about it."

"Thanks…"

"But I'm being serious. I have a reason for asking. I promise."

"It's made me more cautious, I guess," she said finally. "I have to be hyperaware of my surroundings at all times since I can't rely on pain signals. I told you about that rusty tin can when I was a kid, right?"

"Yeah. A few days in the hospital with a high fever. Your foot went slightly purple from infection."

"That's right."

"So worrying about similar things on a day-to-day basis must be tough."

"It is," Tessa admitted. "But it's also made me more observant. I notice things that other people might miss."

"Like what?" Jake asked, his curiosity piqued.

"Subtle changes in a person's behavior," Tessa said, thinking back to some of her past cases. "The way they hold themselves, the way their eyes dart around the room. It's helped me pick up on things that have led to breakthroughs in cases."

"And does this case feel any different?" he asked. "Does this one feel impossible?"

Ooh, he's good, she thought. She couldn't help but smile a bit as she said, "No."

He returned the smile, and for a moment, their eyes locked, and that teasing warmth spread through her again. There was something there; she was sure of it now. But whether or not they'd ever broach *that* topic remained a mystery.

Jake finally cranked the car, turning his eyes away and breaking the gaze. As Jake drove them back to the field office, she was surprised to find a flicker of hope amidst the darkness that surrounded them. She knew they had a long road ahead of them, but with Jake by her side, she was confident they could catch the killer before he struck again.

Because he was right. Together, they'd pretty much been an unstoppable team. And she didn't see that changing anytime soon—if ever.

CHAPTER SEVENTEEN

The fluorescent lights of her office hummed a monotonous lullaby, casting a sterile glow over the files that littered Tessa's desk. She sat in silence with her door closed, her eyes narrowed as she dissected the day's findings like a surgeon with a scalpel, meticulous and precise. The clock ticked away defiantly, reminding her that dawn was only a few hours away. Another day coming and the killer was still at large.

She knew what she was looking for among the papers and records—patterns buried within the crime scenes, the murders themselves, and the lives of the women who'd been killed. Patterns…really, any serial killer case usually came down to a matter of patterns. She flipped through crime scene photos and witness statements, studying each line, each detail. Each victim, affluent in their own right, had met the same grim fate.

"Nothing new," she whispered, pushing back a stray lock of hair that had escaped her ponytail. The frustration was tangible, wrapping around her like the chill of an unwelcome breeze. She leaned back, eyes flitting over the collage of horror spread before her.

She hated that it looked as if they were just going to have the "he hates the wealthy" theory to run with. It seemed over-simplified; not only that but there were a *lot* of wealthy people in Portland. Also, it then got into matters of what, exactly, was considered wealthy.

All three women were wealthy. All three had a connection with pearls. But for the killer to know this, he'd have to be watching them…

It brought her back to one of their original theories…that the killer could be a worker of some kind, someone who was able to come in and out of affluent neighborhoods without seeming strange or uninvited. And if they had to start interviewing every single person who worked in lawn care, landscaping, home maintenance, and so on, this case was never going to end. The killer would take the lives of countless others before they even made the smallest bit of progress.

It was why she'd hoped to make a connection through the lives of the victims, hoping they'd have all shared something else in common. Maybe a gardening club or some sort of bridge club—some social function that would have knit them all together. But so far, there was nothing. She knew Jake was going through these same obstacles in his office, and she could only hope he was seeing things she was missing. He'd asked to simply work it out together, but with the inset of exhaustion and the recent struggles with memories creeping in from her past, she'd opted to work alone for a bit. It was awful to admit, she supposed, but she usually did her best work when she was on her own.

This current situation, however, may prove to be the exception.

She even pulled out her phone and looked to the note, hoping there might be some cryptic clue hidden in what she had dismissed as noting more than a distraction. But she could find nothing new. She knew the letter had not come with prints or any other clues as to its origin; the lab has tested it right away. And apparently, the contents of the letter were going to offer nothing, either.

The weight of unsolved riddles was a millstone around her neck, each cold case file a reminder of promises yet to be fulfilled.

She studied and read and stared, and all it did was make her eyes heavy. Tessa hated to admit *anything* similar to defeat, but she knew if she didn't get a bit of rest, she was going to be useless tomorrow—or, rather, *today*. With a heavy sigh, she got to her feet and slapped off the overhead lights. She then returned to her chair, which groaned in protest as she leaned back. The silence of the office was punctuated only by the distant hum of the air conditioning unit. She knew people were elsewhere in the budling (not many, due to the hour), but she couldn't hear them.

"Twenty minutes," she promised herself, "Just twenty."

Closing her eyes, Tessa instantly felt herself slipping into slumber. Just before drifting off, she sensed that it might be a deep one and wished she'd thought to set an alarm on her phone. But by then, it was too late. The arms of sleep had her, and they were dragging her down.

There was a dream waiting for her as she dozed. It began as a whisper, a gentle pull into the depths of memory. She found herself walking through the corridors of the academy at Quantico, the air thick with the tang of sweat and determination. Younger, more naïve, Tessa walked those halls at her current age and status, her footsteps echoing with the fervor of someone who believed justice could be wrested from the clutches of chaos.

"Flint!" The voice cut through the fog of years, authoritative yet not unkind.

She spun around, the name tag on her chest glinting. There, leaning against the doorway of a classroom, stood a familiar face—a woman named Elle Hackman. Elle, who had been instrumental in helping her work through so many of her own issues, especially those concerning her CIPA-like condition. An instructor and counselor at the academy, Elle had also proven to be a good friend once Tessa had moved to Portland. They'd chatted on the phone, and Elle had even visited last year when she passed through Maine on her way to visit family in Canada.

And now here she was, stuck in this dream…and she was holding a knife. The one true friend from her past at the academy, a threatening presence in this dreamscape.

"Hey there, Flint," she said, brandishing the knife. "You know, if I slip this into your back, right between the vertebrae, you wouldn't feel the pain. But it would sure as hell paralyze you. How would you feel about that?"

“But why would you?” Tessa asked.

“Because everyone needs to feel pain. How are you even human if you’ve never hurt?”

“I’ve hurt plenty. I lost Sarah. I lost—”

“Physical pain is different. The feeling of the blade slipping in under skin and bone. The way a gunshot feels as it blasts through your ribs or collarbone. You need to feel that.”

“But I—”

But Elle turned away, walking down the endless hallway and passing through a door.

"Wait!" Tessa called out, reaching for the figure that represented guidance, stability—a bastion against the storm of uncertainty.

When Tessa reached the doorway, Elle was gone. In her place, there was an open and black abyss. It was cold and unyielding, a void where her fears condensed into tangible horrors. She stumbled through this dreamscape, the edges of reality frayed like worn fabric. The silence here was oppressive, an auditory vacuum that seemed to suck the very breath from her lungs.

"Help me," she whispered, her voice a brittle sound that shattered against the nothingness. But there was no response—only the thick cloak of dread that settled heavily on her shoulders.

Then, without warning, a figure materialized in front of her—a man with no face, just a smooth expanse of skin where features should have been. He moved toward her, silent as a specter, his hands outstretched. In them, he held a pearl necklace, glinting ominously in the non-light.

"Who are you?" Tessa's voice broke the silence, her agent's instinct for interrogation clashing with the primal terror clawing at her psyche. The figure didn't answer, only continued its steady advance.

"Stay back!" she commanded, but her dream self remained rooted to the spot, paralyzed by the chilling recognition of the pearls—the same as those found at the crime scenes.

The faceless man reached her, the pearls looping around her neck with a whisper of menace. They tightened, constricting, each bead pressing into her flesh like a vice. Panic surged, her heart pounding a frenzied rhythm that echoed in her ears.

"Stop! Please!" she gasped, clawing at the implacable string, her nails scraping helplessly against the smooth stones. Her breath came in ragged sobs, the world narrowing to the excruciating pressure around her throat. He was squeezing tighter, tighter…

Tessa jolted awake, her office springing up around her in stark relief.

She was on the floor, a tangle of limbs and spilled files, her heart thundering against her ribs as she fought for air. The remnants of the dream clung to her, a residual terror that made her shudder. Gasping, she pushed herself up, her hands trembling as they wiped the sweat from her brow.

"Christ," she muttered as she went to the light switch and turned the lights back on. She was embarrassed but also shaken by the dream. She didn't have them often, but when she did, they were intense. As she stumbled back to her chair, she realized that while the prospect of the killer taking her life had been awful, the idea of Elle Hackman plunging a knife into her back was even worse.

Elle… she thought.

Tessa wasn't one to read into dreams; she thought people who thought dreams were some sort of subconscious message were a little crazy. Still, she couldn't dislodge Elle from her brain, and she thought that might mean something.

Irritation flared, followed by a resolute determination. Enough was enough. She needed clarity, perspective—something Elle, her makeshift mentor, had always been adept at providing. Tessa checked her pone for the time and was ashamed to find that somehow, it had come to 4:27 in the morning. her nap, which was supposed to have been brief, had lasted nearly fifty minutes.

I should call Elle, she thought. The idea was a pleasing one and seemed to make a tremendous amount of sense. Besides that, it was refreshing to think of Elle as she truly knew her—caring, compassionate, friendly—after seeing her as such a monster in the dream.

They'd not spoken for about three weeks, and that had been a brief phone call. But she also knew that Elle would have no qualms with taking her call to help walk her through the issues she was facing—both professionally and personally.

But maybe not at 4:30 in the morning. She'd wait a few hours to call Elle, and in the meantime, she'd go by Jack's office and see if he'd had any luck. First, though, she needed to go to the breakroom and put on a pot of coffee because the sun hadn't even come up yet, and it was already looking to be a very long day.

CHAPTER EIGHTEEN

The garden behind the field office was barely a garden at all. Some of the agents in the building only jokingly referred to it as such. But just shy of seven in the morning, still without any fresh leads or theories of any kind, Tessa stepped out into the small portion of land on the back western edge of the building. A few wildflowers, four trees, three wooden benches, and a garden gnome someone had ironically placed there greeted her.

Without new breaks in the case, today was going to equate to nothing more than grasping at straws; they'd have to retrace their steps maybe interview people who were so far removed from the victims that it was hard to even think of them as viable sources of information—people like past employees or family members who'd only seen the victims two or three times a year.

So it was Tessa's hope that Elle would be able to unclog her mind—to help her see the case from a fresh perspective through a random FaceTime call.

When Tessa sat down on the bench, a gentle morning breeze wafted across the garden. She'd brought a half-eaten Danish with her, which rested on a napkin in her lap, flaky crumbs scattered around her fingers. She'd also brought a cup of H.Q.'s too-bitter coffee; steam rose from the paper cup of coffee cradled between her hands.

Anxious and nervous, Tessa placed the call. It rang only once before it was answered, and Elle's face appeared, bringing with it an echo of familiarity and comfort.

"Tessa! Good morning to you!"

Elle's brown hair was going slightly gray, and Tessa hated that it was the first thing she noticed. She'd actually noticed it the last time they'd seen one another. It was just such a strange thing to think about someone she'd once viewed with an almost godlike status. Tessa also noted that it looked like Elle was taking the call from her car.

"Hey Elle," Tessa began, a soft smile touching her features, "Is this a bad time? It looks like you're driving."

"I *am* driving. But it's. good time. It's always a good time when you call!"

Tessa's gaze flickered over to the vibrant blossoms that fought bravely against the encroaching shadow of the building. Did she *really* want to start Elle's day with her complaining about a case that sounded *so simple* at its core?

"How's that beach house treating you?" Elle asked. "Though…hold on…that's now where you are, is it?"

"Nope. I'm at work. Behind the field office in the world's saddest little garden. But the beach house, since you asked, is sort of perfect. Therapeutic, even."

"And your partner, Jake Sullivan?"

"What about him?"

"Still just work partners?" Elle asked with a devilish smile. "Not partners in any other way?"

"Just work partners."

"It's a shame. That young man is *yummy."*

"Young man? He's thirty-one, you know."

"Uh-huh. And I'm forty-eight. So yes…he's a *young man.* Anyway, I digress. To what do I owe the pleasure of this call?"

Tessa shifted on the bench, the light breeze teasing strands of her hair. The greenery around her seemed to lean in, eavesdropping on their conversation—a silent audience to her rare moments of vulnerability. She glanced at Elle's image, the pixelated visage of a woman who had seen too much yet never wavered.

"Elle, I need to talk to you about this case I'm on…and some other stuff. But the case first."

"Oh, okay. What about it?"

"We have three victims so far—different backgrounds, different ages, but all on the rich side of the tracks."

"You think it's more than a grudge against the wealthy?"

"I do. He's using pearl necklaces to strangle the women and then leaving pearls behind as a sort of taunt. He's even sent a letter to the bureau, just rubbing out noses in the fact that we have zero leads."

"So the pearls…you think they're symbolic?"

"Maybe. It's sort of a signature for him. Draped around their necks or hands like some grotesque nod to elegance."

"That's a specific choice," Elle murmured, tilting her head slightly. "Pearls symbolize purity, innocence. It could be the killer's way of mocking his victims... or sanctifying them."

"Exactly my thought," Tessa replied, her fingers clenching and unclenching around the phone. "But it's a theory that has gotten us absolutely nowhere."

"Reminds me of my Charleston case," Elle said after a moment, her gaze seeming to pierce through the digital distance. "The perp left keepsakes with his victims as well. A taunt to those who'd find them."

"Did you manage to profile him successfully?" Tessa asked, leaning closer, the bench's wood hard against her back.

"Only when we realized he was reliving a trauma from his childhood," Elle explained. "It gave us the leverage we needed to anticipate his next move. Too two weeks, but we finally got him."

Tessa nodded, absorbing every word. She respected Elle immensely, not just for her analytical prowess but for the human touch she brought to each case. Elle wasn't just profiling criminals; she was dissecting the darkest parts of human nature.

"Your approach is always so unique, Tessa. You see the patterns, connect the dots in ways others don't," Elle praised, and Tessa felt a swell of pride tempered by the weight of responsibility.

"Thank you, Elle. That means a lot coming from you," Tessa replied, a smile tugging at the corners of her mouth despite the grim subject matter.

"Trust your instincts," Elle advised. "They've led you right before. Probably more times than you know."

"That's just the thing…my instincts seem to be frozen. I don't know where to go, where to turn, what to look for. And I think it's because of the other thing I want to tell you about. And I'd really appreciate it if you could respond with something other than 'go see a shrink.'"

"I promise nothing. But go ahead."

"I'm being bombarded with memories from my past. Things about my medical condition and about Sarah."

"Yikes. That's a lot."

"It is. And I know it sounds like a lame excuse, but all of these things started coming just a day or two before this case, and I don't know if…I don't know if it's just too much to handle. I won't quit or give up—you know that—but I just needed…I don't know, some guidance, I suppose."

Elle was all serious now, the smirk gone from her face as she continued to drive but also paid attention to the call. The phone camera was stationary, making Tessa assume it was mounted on a car holder on Elle's dashboard.

"Okay, so if I can't give the answer I want, which you specifically asked me not to, I'm not sure how to answer. But if you truly won't give up, I think you need to let your supervisor know about these personal issues. You're brilliant on a case, Tessa, but I also know how you can sometimes be a closed book emotionally. You need to figure out which takes precedence right now: the case or your personal demons."

Deep down, Tessa had known this was the answer. But it took hearing Elle say it for it to truly sink in. "Yeah, I know."

"You'll be okay, Tessa."

Tessa nodded and then asked a question that had been on her mind but not one she'd intended to ask Elle.

"Elle…do you think the bureau ever be persuaded to re-open an old case?"

Elle's seasoned eyes softened with understanding, recognizing the veiled reference laced in Tessa's question. She knew Tessa wasn't merely asking about any case; she was speaking of the one that had haunted her for years—Sarah's disappearance.

"Re-opening a case depends on many factors, Tess," Elle replied cautiously. "New evidence, fresh leads..." She trailed off, weighing her words. "I have no idea what the official stance would be now. But it never hurts to ask. Sometimes, all it takes is the right person asking the right questions."

Tessa absorbed this, a glint of hope sparking in her otherwise weary eyes. A cardinal flitted onto a nearby branch, its vibrant red plumage stark against the muted colors of the garden. It was a burst of life amidst the stagnation, a silent encouragement to pursue what seemed impossible.

"Thank you, Elle. There's no new evidence, of course, but…maybe if I look into it on my own time, I can find something.." Tessa's voice was firmer now, the determination that had briefly wavered was steadying itself once more.

Tessa could sense the call coming to an end. After all, she had a case to solve, and Elle was out on her way to start her day. But Elle had a few more encouraging words for her. "Remember, Tessa, you've cracked cases people said were uncrackable. And I'm sure you'll crack this one, too."

"Thanks," she said with no real emotion.

"Listen, Tessa. You've spent what…two and a half years now finding light in the darkest alleys of human depravity. Don't forget how far you've come and what you're capable of. I've told you on more than one occasion that I keep my ears open, and I hear about how well you're doing. You've cracked cases much harder than this one.

A smile quivered at the edge of Tessa's lips, her heart buoyed by the praise. It was easy to lose oneself in the labyrinth of one's failures, but Elle's reminder was a beacon, casting light on Tessa's past triumphs.

"Thanks for this, Elle. I appreciate it."

"I don't know much it helped, but…"

"It helped more than you might think."

"Good," Elle nodded with finality. "And don't hesitate to reach out again if you need to bounce more ideas or just talk. You're not alone in this. Remember that."

"I know. Bye, Elle."

Tessa ended the call with a newfound vigor coursing through her veins. As she gathered up her coffee and Danish, her phone buzzed. The caller display told her that it was Jake…her 'yummy' partner, apparently.

"Hey, Jake," she answered.

"He's hit again, Tessa," Jake said, his voice was thick was anger and concern. "We've got a fourth victim."

CHAPTER NINETEEN

The morning was already starting to stretch away as Tessa and Jake arrived at the scene of the fourth murder. They were both quiet and stoic as they approached the long string of crime scene tape. She supposed she was still tired, but she had managed to push that sensation away. This time, the victim had been found in a townhouse rather than a huge, elaborate home. The chain of townhomes situated side by side on the property *were* very nice, though, the location sitting right on the edge of one of the more coveted neighborhoods in the city. In fact, it was just a mile away from the Flowers' residence.

Tessa ducked under the crime scene tape looped off in front of the front door, with Jake following closely behind. Coming in through the front door, it was easy to spot the victim right away. It was a woman who appeared to be no older than forty, was all the way across the foyer; she was sprawled out in an elegant recliner, her head tilted up, her body limp.

A single cop was standing in the small space where the open-space living room merged with the kitchen. "So far, it looks like the same M.O. as the others," he said. "Then again, I've only been here for about five minutes."

As they stepped further into the house, Tessa took note of the two policeman and the plainclothes detective on the other side of the room. It looked like they were comparing notes. Everyone seemed to be steering clear of the body, likely waiting for forensics to show up.

"Let's see what we're dealing with," Tessa said as she passed through the foyer and stepped into the living room.

"Well, her name is the lone cop," Jake said. "Thirty-seven, an interior designer for some pretty big names."

"And she's living in a townhouse?"

"For now. We just got word that she's got a plot of land out by the lake…building a house."

"So she had money, then," Tessa remarked.

She continued to look the place over. Everything was elaborately decorated and clean. The entire place smelled of lavender and vanilla. She scanned the body—the fourth victim in a string of murders that seemed to have the entire local P.D. and the FBI holding their collective breath. She noted the pearls right away, a string of them draped around the victim's neck. They seemed very out of place given that she was wearing a beautiful silk pajama top and the matching shorts.

“There’s the indention of the necklace,” Jake said, pointing to the flared, red ring around her neck, the shape of the pearls clearly defined. “The same as the other three.”

"Not quite…”

"What am I missing?"

"The pearls... they're doubled this time. Two strands," she observed, her fingers hovering just above the glistening beads, careful not to disturb the scene. "Before, it was always a single strand, wasn't it?"

“Yeah.”

“So maybe there’s some sort of symbolism here.”

"Or he's escalating," Jake suggested, his brow furrowed.

"Exactly." Tessa's mind whirred as she contemplated the implications. "Doubling the pearls could mean doubling the message he's trying to send. Or it's a sign that he's growing bolder, more confident."

"Confidence can lead to mistakes," Jake pointed out.

"Let's hope." Tessa's thoughts churned with the profiles of known offenders, patterns of criminal behavior, and psychological analysis. It was a jigsaw puzzle with too many missing pieces, and every new murder was a stark reminder of the stakes.

But this killer was meticulous, leaving behind a scant trail at best. He knew they were struggling, and he was still taunting them. He'd left clues, and now he was escalating things.

So maybe he's starting to worry that we’re on to him, Tessa hoped.

"This is recent,” Tessa said, nodding to the marks on her neck. “Who found her?”

“Her cleaning lady,” the plainclothes detective said. He was an older, African American gentleman and he looked just as pissed as Tessa felt. “She’s outside speaking to two officers right now.”

“And she didn’t see anyone strange or out of place?”

“She says she didn’t,” the detective said.

“I’ll go talk to her,” Jake said.

“And I'll stay here a bit longer, see if I can pick up on anything we might have missed," Tessa said. Her gaze remained on the lifeless eyes of Alice Peterson. In those depths, she searched for answers, for a clue that would lead them one step closer to the monster they were hunting.

Tessa crouched by the recliner. Without touching the body, she looked at Alice's hands and forearms. There were no cuts or bruises. And everything in the house was immaculate. In other words, there had been no struggle. The killer had caught her unaware, strangled her, and then laid her out in the recliner.

Tessa then looked to the spot just above the crook of the elbow, where the injection marks had been on the other three victims. It was the same case here. A barely visible prick and a slightly inflamed, red area.

She thought of how close together the townhouses were. Maybe if they canvassed the area, they'd find someone who'd spotted a stranger—someone not usually in the area. Based on the angry shade of red at Alice's throat, she didn't think more than three or four hours had passed since the murder.

She was probably losing her life while you were napping in your office, she told herself. She knew this could potentially be true but also knew she couldn't allow herself to dwell on that for now.

Two strings of pearls this time. But why? Was there something different about Alice Peterson? Did it have to do with where she lived? Did it maybe have something to do with the big move she was about to make into a from-scratch lake house?

She continued to look the body over—as well as the chair and the carpeted floor. She looked high and low, under furniture and behind the cushions of the couch against the wall. She checked the kitchen and everywhere she could without moving the body…but she found no pearls intentionally left behind.

Frustrated, she figured she could head outside and start speaking to Alice's neighbors to see if they could provide any information. As she stepped back outside, she came down Alice Peterson's stairs just as Jake was stepping away from a young redhead sitting on the curb with a policeman—apparently Alice's cleaner.

"Was she any help?"

"Not in any big ways. She said the front door was unlocked when she got there, which was unusual. She said she always had to knock because Alice always kept her door locked. And she also said she *knows* Alice wore pearl necklaces on occasion, but not just around the house."

Tessa nodded, doing everything she could not to lose herself to the building anger and frustration. This should *not* be this hard. They were quickly coming to the point where more agents would have to be assigned. Four dead now…it was the sort of thing a city started to notice. And once news of this serial killer made a bigger impact in headlines and social media, the chances of him getting away increased. It was like a warning—more attention meant it was time to hit the road.

And she'd be damned if she'd let this one get away.

"We should have this guy by now, Jake."

"I agree. But we're doing everything we can."

"Are we?" Tessa's voice cracked, betraying the ironclad composure she fought so hard to maintain. "Because it doesn't feel like it's enough. Not when they keep dying."

Jake fell silent, knowing there were no words of comfort that could penetrate the fortress of Tessa's self-doubt.

"Let's canvass the area," she said. "Someone around here had to have seen something. And if that fails, then we're just going to have to accept that Lawson will have to put more agents on this."

In that moment, as if specifically designed by the universe itself, Tessa's phone rang. The caller display revealed that it was Lawson.

"Speak of the devil," she said. She then answered, trying not to sound as frustrated as she truly felt. "This is Flint."

"Flint, it's Lawson. Is Sullivan there with you?"

"He is."

"Put this on speaker, then. Quickly."

Tessa did as she was asked, leaning against her car. She dared to hope this call might actually provide a bit of good news for once.

"You're on speaker," Tessa said.

"Good. Listen…it took longer than we'd hoped, but we've secured the warrant for Crabtree's safe. I want you two there right now. I understand you're both doing all you can, but this entire case is getting out of hand."

"Understood," Tessa replied as adrenaline started spiking through her. "We're on our way."

***

They covered the distance to Crabtree's Fine Jewelry in silence as they both tried sorting out the case details in their own respective minds, and in their own ways. But as soon as they were out of the car, having parked behind two patrol cars, there was a thrumming electricity between them as they once again felt the promise of a big lead right around the corner.

They entered into the store and Tessa couldn't help but looked directly at the glass she'd shattered two days ago. Crabtree hadn't replaced it yet, but he'd removed the inventory and moved it elsewhere. As for Crabtree himself, he was nowhere to be seen.

They moved to the back of the store, where two policemen and a locksmith were all pressed against the back wall. Crabtree was absent here as well, and Tessa wondered if he'd simply refused to be present for such an invasion of his business.

Tessa watched the locksmith's hands dance with practiced precision, coaxing the stubborn lock to yield its secrets. The air was thick with tension, as if the very walls anticipated the revelations to come.

"Almost there," the locksmith grunted, his tools clicking in quick succession. Tessa did her best to calm her excitement, reminding herself that they could easily open this safe and find absolutely nothing of consequence.

With a final twist of the lock and an expert placement of a small drill bit, the safe door groaned open. The locksmith made a whistling sound as he stepped away to let Tessa and Jake look inside.

Stacks of cash lay unassumingly next to bags of white powder that could only be cocaine—silent yet screaming evidence of illicit dealings. There were a few rings and a diamond in a plastic bag without a case. It was stunning and, if she had to guess, was worth somewhere in the low six figures.

But it was the pearl necklaces, each one placed with an eerie grace, that drew Tessa's focus.

They were the killer's calling card, the thread that linked the victims together.

"Damn, look at these," Jake murmured, reaching out but not touching, knowing better than to disturb the scene.

Tessa's eyes were drawn to something else, though. There were three necklaces sitting in the safe, but one of them had a tag attached to it. Two names had been scrawled on the tag. On was familiar and the other was not.

"Regina Flowers," she said, reading the first name.

"The second victim," Jake commented. "Why the hell would her name be on this necklace?"

"No idea. But that second name…it seems familiar. Have you heard it before?"

Jake read it out loud. "Ethan Miller. I don't think so."

Tessa looked to the cops, her heart ramping up a bit. This was a huge lead, maybe big enough to close this case. "Can one of you run the name from your car?"

“Yeah, I’m on it,” one of the cops said. He hurried out of the back office, clearly exhilarated to be a part of such a discovery.

"The tag, though," Jake said. "It looks like the same sort of tag you'd see in stores like this. Jewelry stores, antiques stores, whatever. Something you'd put a price on."

“I wonder if maybe Crabtree had set it aside and knew these two people would be interested. That *could* make sense. We know that Regina liked pearls.”

“Crabtree could tell us.”

“Where *is* he, anyway?” Tessa asked, looking back to the locksmith and the remaining cop.

“He was *pissed,”* the locksmith said. “He locked me out of the shop until the cops arrived. And even then he refused to open the safe despite the warrant.”

“So he’s at the precinct,” the cop said. “And if he didn’t calm down, I wouldn’t be surprised if he’s in a holding cell by now.”

As Tessa’s eyes went back to the necklaces in the safe, the other cop came hurrying back through the store. They could hear his heavy footfalls approaching.

“We got a hit,” he said. “Ethan Miller is a sec offender from a few years back. He’s also got a breaking and entering and a few drunk and disorderlies in his past. Been in jail twice for small infractions. The most time he served was three months."

"And his name just happens to be linked to a murder victim," Tessa said. "On a symbol, the murderer is leaving behind, at that."

“Got an address?” Jake asked the cop.

“I was pretty sure you’d ask,” the cop said, offering Jake a scrap slip of paper where he’d written the address down.

“Want us to bag all this stuff?” the first cop asked.

"Yeah, and I'd put out an arrest warrant for Crabtree on the drugs," Tessa said. "Take pictures and seal off the office of first. This all may come back into play depending on how things go with Ethan Miller. Thanks for your hard work, everyone.”

As she and Jake hurried out of the store with the next suspect’s address, she couldn't shake the image of the pearls, each one a mark of death. It gnawed at her, the idea that this Ethan Miller might hold the key to stopping the carnage. His history painted a grim picture for sure, but was he the killer or just another taunting dead-end?

CHAPTER TWENTY

Morning had officially given way to noon as Tessa and Jake arrived at the address for Ethan Miller. He lived in a neighborhood that felt forgotten—not necessarily economically slighted, but the sort of neighborhood that felt as if it were holding its breath. No one on the streets, the lawns dying and slightly overgrown. As for Miller's house, it looked tailor-made for a man with a shady past. The white vinyl siding was in need of washing and the single flower pot on the porch steps was faded, the plants long dead and forgotten.

"Looks like something out of a ghost story," Jake muttered beside her, his breath clouding the space between them.

As they approached, Tessa found herself again unsettled by the eerie quiet and calm of the neighborhood. They walked onto the porch—which, like the siding, was also in need of some love and care—and Jake knocked on the door. The sound seemed to echo through the entire street.

Moments later, the door creaked open, revealing man that looked to be middle aged. His hair was unkempt, his eyes wary and guarded. "Yeah?" he asked in a haggard voice. "Who're you?"

"We're looking for Ethan Miller," Jake said. "Is that you?"

"Yes, but who are you?" His scowl showed signs that the man was untrusting by default.

Jake too the lead, showing his badge. "Agents Sullivan and Flint, FBI. We need to ask you a few questions."

For a split second, Tessa thought Miller was going to slam the door in their faces. He moved to do it for a moment but seemed to think better of it at the last moment.

"FBI? What the hell for?"

"Just some routine questions regarding events in your neighborhood," Tessa said smoothly, though nothing about this felt routine. "One of your neighbors may be in a bit of trouble, but we're trying to get a better picture from others on the street."

She saw right away that the lie had eased him a bit. He grinned briefly and chuckled. "I can think of at least three folks on this street that are always up to trouble."

"Mind if we come in?" Jake asked, his tone conversational, but his posture professional and alert. “It won’t take long and we’d really rather not have any snooping neighbors spot us and tip of our suspect.”

Miller hesitated, the grin leaving his mouth to be replaced by that slight frown of distrust. After a few seconds, he stepped aside and said, “Come in.”

The interior of his home matched the exterior: dark, dingy, with a faint odor of neglect. Tessa's gaze swept across the room, cataloging details—the stains on the carpet, the stack of magazines by the recliner, the faint outline where pictures once hung but had since been removed.

As she and Jake settled into the threadbare couch, Tessa began her probing. And now that they were inside his house, she was perfectly fine with letting up from the ruse they’d fed him outside.

"We found your name on a tag with a pearl necklace in Victor Crabtree's safe," she said, watching his reaction closely. She pitched her voice to sound casual, but her mind raced with the possibilities. “There were two names, actually. Yours and the name of a woman who was recently killed.”

Fury exploded in his eyes as he stood at the other end of the couch closest to the door. “You said this was about a neighbor.”

“Would you have let us in if we led with what Agent Flint just told you?” Jake said.

“Get out!”

“Sure,” Tessa said. “As soon as you explain that tag and your associations with both Victor Crabtree and Regina Flowers.”

Miller's face paled, a vein throbbing at his temple. "I don't know what you're talking about," he stammered, but his agitation was palpable. Tessa saw his fists clench and unclench, his eyes darting between her and Jake.

"Is there a reason your name would be associated with Mrs. Flowers?" Jake asked, leaning forward slightly as if inviting confidence.

"Never heard of her," Miller snapped, shifting uneasily in his chair. Tessa could feel the tension coiling in the room, the sense that something critical was on the verge of snapping.

“And what about Crabtree?” Tessa asked.

“Don’t know him. He’s the guy that owns the big jewelry store, right?”

That’s right. Now, Mr. Miller..." Tessa continued, her voice a mixture of steel and silk. "We're trying to piece together a very disturbing puzzle. Your cooperation could make all the difference."

But even as she spoke, Tessa knew they were inching closer to a precipice, one wrong step away from an irreversible fall. Miller's discomfort was a tangible thing now, filling the space like a third person.

“I don’t know what to tell you,” he said.

Tessa could see him doing his best to come up with a way out of this. And the way he’d taken just a single step back while still clenching and unclenching his fist made her also wonder if he was considering a physical confrontation. His eyes were like shards of glass, hard and reflecting a story he wasn't telling.

"Mr. Miller," Tessa pressed, taking a deliberate step closer, "your name was found connected to one of four victims. That's not a coincidence we can ignore. So you either explain this now, or we *will* arrest you for suspicion of murder.”

“Murder? Are you serious?” His voice boomed and he was suddenly taking that step back toward them. She felt Jake tense next to her and then get to his feet to match Miller’s posture.

"I said I don’t know this victim…this Flowers woman!"

"Easy, Miller," Jake cautioned, but his partner's instincts were already firing on all cylinders. The man before them was unraveling, his façade cracking under the weight of their questions. “We just need to—”

"Get out! Get out of my house!" Miller surged forward, as if daring Jake to start something. His entire frame was shaking with rage. It was a raw, primal outburst, the kind that comes when someone is cornered, desperate.

He’s angry, sure, Tessa thought. *But he’s also scared.*

Tessa remained where she was on the ratty couch. She knew fear could be a powerful motivator for both confession and violence. As an agent, she had seen it lead to both. And she’d also seen guilt in the eyes of men, like a slick sheen. She could see it now, in the way Miller’s gaze flickered, the sweat on his brow, the pulse throbbing visibly at his throat. The pearls had been the whisper of evidence they needed, but Miller's reaction screamed confession.

"Miller, we're not leaving until—"

But her words were cut short as he reached out, grabbing at Jake’s arm and attempting to wrench him toward the door. His strength was surprising; a coiled spring of fury unleashed without warning.

“I said *get out!”*

"Damn it," Tessa muttered, shifting into a defensive stance. She reached for her Glock, her mind racing through protocols and contingencies. Her training kicked in, muscle memory guiding her actions even as her brain screamed caution.

Jake did his best to reverse the sloppy hold, but Miller's fear and anger added to his strength. Both men fought for control of the situation as Tessa got to her feet and placed her hands on Miller's shoulders. She intended to simply pull his left arm back at a hard angle and then bring it up in a reverse armbar.

But Miller was a tempest of aggression, his bulk surprisingly agile as he swatted her away and then swung a meaty fist back toward Jake. It connected with Jake's jaw, sending him sprawling across the threadbare carpet.

Tessa's mind raced. She could pull the Glock, or she could fight. The Glock could either neutralize things and end this, or it could lead to a fatal situation. So she'd just have to fight.

As it turned out, she was going to *have* to, as Miller threw out another of his slow but devastating punches. Tessa sidestepped it easily enough and when Miller tottered a bit on the follow-through, Tessa wrapped both arms around his neck while also bringing her right knee up and planting it firmly in his spine.

"Calm down, Miller!" Her words were ironclad, backed by the full force of her authority. Yet, Miller still fought, his legs pushing back against her and nearly making her stumble back. She kept her hold around his neck. If she had to choke the bastard out, then so be it.

She knew she could do it. This wasn't just about muscle; it was about momentum, leverage, and the will to remain standing when your body screamed surrender. She felt the adrenaline surge, her senses sharpened. Every lesson she'd ever learned about self-defense, every drill she'd practiced until her muscles ached—they all funneled into this moment.

When he attempted to run backwards to slam her into the wall, she planted her feet. And although his weight continued to push her back, she used his reverse momentum to raise her forearms up closer to his jaw while also clenching the hold in. She thought this would be the end of it, but the desperation in Miller knew no bounds.

He rocked his head back, slamming the back of his skull into her forehead. The sound was awful, and for a moment, white flares sailed across her vision. She loosed her grip not because she felt any pain but because of the absurd and unexpected nature of the attack.

He attempted to wrestle free of her, but just as he had nearly escaped, Tessa drove her right foot into the back of his knee. Miller howled, and when he went to the floor, Tessa again cinched the hold in around his neck. She could feel the pulse of his carotid beneath her forearm, the heat of his breath against her skin as she fell on top of him, pinning him to the floor.

"Try anything, and I'll put you to sleep," she hissed into his ear, aware of how close his teeth were to her flesh.

"Let go... you bitch!" Miller spat, his voice ragged with pain and defiance.

Miller bucked, a last-ditch effort to free himself, but Tessa rode out the wave, her entire being focused on maintaining control. She could hear Jake getting to his feet behind her, could sense his presence rejoining the fray.

"Got your cuffs?" she called over her shoulder, not daring to loosen her grasp on Miller.

"Right here," Jake grunted, moving into her line of sight, his face set in grim determination despite the swelling already blooming along his jawline. He fell in beside Tessa and helped her pull his arms down against the wild and screaming protests from Miller. He snapped the handcuffs around Miller's wrists, the click resounding like the closing of a book—a chapter ending, another beginning.

And with that click came a fragile hope: they had the killer. They'd caught him—Ethan Miller, the link in a chain of deaths, each adorned with a pearl necklace. But doubt gnawed at her; it was never this straightforward, was it?

"Let's get him to H.Q. We'll sort it out there," she said, finally releasing her hold on Miller.

"Good work, Tessa," Jake said, meeting her eyes with an exhausted nod.

"Teamwork," she corrected, allowing herself a small smile, feeling the weight of uncertainty lift—for now.

Jake hauled Miller to is feet with a bit more force that was necessary, releasing some of the anger and pain form the blow he'd taken to the jaw. And though Miller bucked and cursed the entire way, they got him into the car. As Jake got in behind the wheel and started the engine, Miller's reactions continued to grow the hope within Tessa that this was it…tat Miller was their man and this case was just a simple interrogation from being closed.

CHAPTER TWENTY ONE

The sterile air of the interrogation room at FBI headquarters hummed with tension, charged like the ominous quiet before a storm. Tessa's eyes bore into Ethan Miller, who sat cuffed across the table from her and Jake. The bruise on Jake's jaw was darkening, a souvenir from the encounter that had escalated far more rapidly than they had anticipated.

"Let's not waste time, Miller," Tessa began, her voice a controlled calm that belied the adrenaline still coursing through her veins from their earlier altercation. "We know you're involved in this. Maybe the killer, maybe not. And you can make it *much* easier on yourself by just spilling it all right now."

She was aware that there were at least a dozen people standing behind the two-way glass on the right side of the room. SAIC Lawson was among them; Tessa could feel her superior's unseen gaze through the glass and it somehow made her even more confident that she could crack Miller.

Miller's eyes darted between Tessa and Jake, the weight of their stares pressing down upon him. His Adam's apple bobbed in a nervous swallow, and when he spoke, it was with a desperation that clawed its way through the bravado he attempted to project. "I'm no killer," he asserted, licking his cracked lips. "And I have no idea who Regina Flowers is."

"Then why did we find your name on a tag, with *her* name, strapped to a pearl necklace?"

Tessa had taken note of how some of the rage had gone sliding right out of him as they'd arrived at the field office. And by the time they started marching him down the halls, sterile and featureless, all the fight was out of him. She'd seen it before and knew it was usually because seeing the interior of an FBI office was *totally* different than being rolled into a basic police precinct. It felt more official—more dangerous.

And that was sowing in Miller's face as he continued to stare at them. He was shaken, and Tessa was pretty sure he was going to do everything he could to get out of this mess—even if it required telling the truth.

"Because," Miller finally said. "You were right about one thing. I *have* been working with Crabtree."

"Doing what exactly?" Jake pressed.

"Jewelry," Miller admitted with a resigned sigh, as if the word carried the weight of all his sins. "Crabtree hires me to steal high-end stuff from people who don't really know it's high-end. Mostly from antique shops, sometimes from people directly. He pays me for the theft, and then I also get a percentage of what he sells them for. He's got the connections, sells them to those willing to pay top dollar."

"And he makes money off of this?" Jake asked.

Miller laughed, albeit a bit nervously. "I've seen him sell a bracelet that the original peddler was selling for three hundred for over two grand. So yeah…it works."

"High-paying customers," she mused aloud, her tone even. "And you never asked questions?"

"Other than 'what's my cut?' no, I never asked anything. It's a pretty simple process."

Tessa's mind was a whirling dervish of thoughts—calculating, considering, mapping out the implications of Miller's confession. If this was all true, it wasn't the neat conclusion to their case she had hoped for. And the so-called confession would be easy enough to check out; it would just take some grilling of Victor Crabtree.

"Do you happen to know if Crabtree already had particular buyers in mind when you would bring him back these stolen pieces?"

"I don't know for sure, but I always thought so. Like, there would be some jobs where he'd be very specific about what he wanted and then he'd send me out."

"How's that work?" Tessa asked. "Tell us, step by step."

Now that the confession had started, the rest seemed to come out easier. Tessa thought Miller looked almost relieved to finally be airing it all out, even if he knew it was going to result in at least some sort of criminal charges against him. Anything was better than multiple counts of murder, after all.

"So, he'd call me and say something like 'I need a diamond ring, sapphire, by the end of the week. So I'd do some digging. Sometimes I'd drive as far as three or four hours away, depending on what he needed. And as long as I found what he needed and brought it to him on time, he was happy and so was I."

"How long has this been going on?" Jake asked.

Miller thought about it for a moment and shrugged. “Six or seven months, I guess.”

He was now speaking as if none of this was a big deal—as if he’d forgotten that the entire reason they’d come for him was because of a series of murders. Tessa noted Jake's swollen jaw clenching in frustration, but Tessa remained outwardly impassive. She needed to tread carefully; any hint of disbelief could push Miller into retreating behind a wall of silence. Inwardly, she cataloged every flicker of expression, every hesitant pause to ensure he was being truthful.

And so far, she thought he was.

"Alright, Miller," she said, setting her pen down with deliberate slowness. "For now, let’s say we buy this. We’d still have to keep you hear because you just admitted to quite a few different crimes. And as we keep digging into this, if we find out you’re lying—”

"I ain't," Miller interrupted quickly, too quickly, his voice climbing an octave. "You'll see. Talk to Crabtree—he'll back it all up. And if I have to, I can…shit, I can give you the names of some of the places I stole from."

He seemed deflated after saying this, a man who had officially shown his hand. The realization of the amount of trouble he could get into seemed to sink in.

“I think we might just do that,” Tessa said as she stood up. “We may be seeing you again soon, Mr. Miller.”

Miller nodded, his eyes now downcast as he realized he wasn’t going anywhere anytime soon.

As Tessa and Jake exited the interrogation room, she cast one last glance at Miller through the one-way mirror. His slumped posture and the sheen of sweat on his brow painted a picture of defeat, but Tessa knew better than to take it at face value. There might still be more pieces to this puzzle, and Victor Crabtree may have them.

***

The precinct where Crabtree was being detained was just a nine-minute drive from the field office. As Jake drove, Tessa called ahead and requested a meeting with Crabtree.

“Oh, that’ll be fun,” the arresting officer told her on the phone. “Just a heads up, this man is screaming and cussing more than some of the more hardened gang members I’ve interacted with. He’s fiery for an old jeweler, that’s for sure.”

And he's going to be even worse when he realizes that Miller just gave him up, Tessa thought. *If Miller is telling the truth, of course.*

Arriving at the precinct was a bit jarring; moving from the more open and somehow more oppressive feel of the formal confines of the field office to a busy and somewhat cluttered police precinct was like stepping out of a flattened meadow and into a looming jungle. The officer in charge of Crabtree met them in the lobby and led them through the precinct. All eyes were on them as news of new developments in the case had already started to spread.

The officer led them to the rear interrogation room, just across the hall from the entrance to the holding cells. He opened the door for them an as they entered, he closed it and made his leave. The interrogation room was a cold, sterile box. Tessa watched as Jake paced the length of the narrow space, his footsteps an echo of the tension thrumming between them. Across the table, Victor Crabtree sat with his hands chained to the heavy metal ring in the center.

"Alright, Mr. Crabtree," Tessa began, her voice steady despite the fatigue that clawed her again. "We need you to confirm what Ethan Miller has been telling us."

His eyes went wide with alarm for a moment…and it was all Tessa needed to know. He could deny knowing Miller and that they had some sort of partnership all he wanted. But that look of shock—of a secret being brought to the light—had just exposed him.

"My God, what has that imbecile been saying?"

"Enough," Tessa said. "So just level with us because to be honest, if this is all eh says it is, I'm still rather annoyed that this is all sidelining us from trying to catch a killer."

"How is my jewelry store connected to a murderer?" Crabtree asked with venom in his voice.

As patiently as she could, Tessa told him about the tag on the necklace—the tag that bore both Miller's name as well as that of Regina Flowers. And as the entirety of the situation became apparent to him, Crabtree went slightly pale. Much like the fight coming out of Miller, Tessa could also see the venom and stubbornness leave Crabtree.

"So how did you know Regina Flowers?" Jake asked.

"She…she was a customer. Fairly regular. And she came into my store a few weeks ago, asking for a very particular sort of pearl necklace."

"And you had Miller steal it?"

Crabtree grimaced for a moment, as if the idea of admission pained him. But he nodded and said, “Yes.”

“He said this little partnership has been going on for about seven months,” Jake said. “Is that right?”

“Yes.”

Tessa felt a shock of disappointment. She had hoped, no—she had needed Crabtree to challenge Miller's story, to give them a reason to dig deeper. But instead, here was another layer of this sordid tapestry, confirming their worst fears. They weren't dealing with a cold-blooded killer, but rather a petty criminal partnership.

However…maybe there was something to be gained from it.

"Have you recently sold several pearl necklaces to anyone all at once?" Tessa asked, probing for a connection, any connection, to the string of murders.

Crabtree thought about it for a moment before answering. “Recently, no. And if I did in the past…I can’t recall. Pearls are quite popular, after all.”

“Okay…well, this little partnership you had with Ethan Miller…is it the first time you’ve associated with criminals?”

He scowled at her for a moment, apparently seeing this as a jab. “To this extent, yes.”

“The bricks of cocaine suggest otherwise.”

“It sort of goes hand in hand,” Crabtree said sadly. “Same crowd and all…”

Tessa looked to Jake, trying to soften her eyes as if trying to telepathically communicate—to apologize in advance for what she was about say.

“Mr. Crabtree, I’m going to level with you here, okay? We have four dead women on our hands, all strangled to death with pearl necklaces. They are either symbolic to him or he’s using them as something of a calling card. If you can think of anyone you’ve come into contact with over the past year or so that has come asking for several pearl necklaces or—”

"Hold on," Crabtree said, suddenly sitting upright in the chair. The chains of the cuffs clinked against the table. "There was a gentleman…I can't remember how long ago this was. But he came in, asking if I had any South Sea pearls."

“What are those?” Jake asked.

"South sea pearls are known for holding several different lusters…all taking on the colors of shells: gold, cream, or pink. They aren't explicitly rare—not as rare as Tahitian pearls, for example—but they can be very difficult to find."

"And did you have any for this man that has suddenly come to your mind?" Tessa asked.

"I did not, but I told him I could find them for him. He was *very* upset about it and insisted he didn't need me to order them. But then the same fellow came back in a few weeks later and apologized for his behavior. That day, he bought a necklace. Pearls…though I don't know what kind. He said he was a bit of a collector. And if I recall…"

He stopped here, thinking deeply, as if trying to pull the memories from the depths of his mind.

"What is it?" Tessa asked. She felt a stirring of excitement and revelation but wasn't quite ready to get her hopes up.

"He was quite knowledgeable about pearls. I asked if he was a dealer himself, but he insisted he was just a collector—that he appreciated their beauty and how they were formed into such amazing items from such a basic and natural process."

"Okay, and why does this man stick out to you specifically…other than losing his temper and apologizing for it later?"

"Well…not many people are *that* knowledgeable about pearls. I mean, he knew things I didn't know. It was a strange conversation indeed."

"And you say you did sell him a necklace that day?"

"I did, yes."

"When was this?" Jake asked.

"I…I can't be sure. Maybe two months ago?"

"With him buying something from you, is there any chance at all that you have his address or a phone number?"

"No. I'm sorry. But…I believe he did pay with a credit card."

Tessa and Jake locked eyes. Everything seemed to be slipping into place now. "Mr. Crabtree, we need access to your records. We need to find this man's information. With a credit card transaction, we can get everything we need."

Crabtree nodded, all the toxicity to his demeanor now gone. He now seemed almost dizzy, trying to catch up with the hugeness of what he'd just revealed.

"I'll get someone to get you out of those cuffs," Jake said.

He left the room, leaving Tessa and Victor Crabtree sitting alone, across the table from one another, with the heaviness of the most promising lead yet hanging in the air between them.

CHAPTER TWENTY TWO

Cassidy hadn't even bothered going home after her shift at the Rise and Shine diner was over at noon. She'd worked the morning shift, waking up very early, so she'd missed her morning run. So she decided to sneak the run in directly after work, before getting home to shower and get ready for her online English Lit course.

That's what led her to her favorite trail at 12:25 in the afternoon, a route she was intimately familiar with. Her breaths came in rhythmic exhalations, each step a testament to her will to keep fit and clear-minded. The gated community offered an illusion of security, but recent events had pierced that bubble of safety like a needle through silk.

There was just her and the voices in her earbuds—and the steady beat of her feet on the dirt. "...and when you really look at the evidence," murmured the voice from the podcast she was listening to, "you see that every clue points to a pattern we've failed to notice until now."

Cassie was an avid follower of true crime podcasts, a way to keep her mind engaged while her body worked the trail. It was her ritual, a slice of time for herself before the day's responsibilities ensnared her.

Her finger danced over the screen of her phone, secured in the band around her arm. The current episode had finished, and she looked for another distraction. And that perfect little balance of time was what allowed her to hear the sound from just slightly behind her. Leaves rustled unnaturally behind her, not the gentle whispering dance performed by a passing breeze or small woodland animal but a heavier, purposeful movement.

Cassie's heartbeat, already elevated from the jog, spiked. She had read about the recent murders in the city just this morning as the breakfast rush had died down at the diner. She'd read how they seemed random, yet all too close to home. Instinctively, she increased her pace, the squelch of her sneakers against the moist earth quickening.

Probably just a deer, she tried to convince herself. Deer *had* been popping up in the city here and there, pushed out of their more natural habitats further north by logging and the development of homes and neighborhoods. Still, her eyes darted to the periphery, seeking the comfort of another jogger, a dog walker—any sign of life that might dispel the growing dread blooming in her chest. But the path remained desolately empty, framed by the whispering trees that now seemed like silent accomplices to her fear.

She attempted to focus on the pounding of her heart, the burn in her legs, anything to anchor herself back to reality and away from the terror that gnawed at her thoughts. Because she had opted not to start another podcast in order to better hear whatever was taking place along the edge of the forest beside her, she could hear it as the rustling persisted, keeping pace with her own movements. A cold shiver ran down her spine despite the warmth of the exercise, her mind unable to shake off the idea that she was no longer alone on the trail.

Cassie's heartbeat synchronized with the thrumming in her ears, a relentless drum that seemed to be getting louder with each passing second. She tried to steady her breathing, focusing on the rhythmic pattern of her strides, when suddenly, the trail ahead skewed into an unexpected turn.

It was then that a hooded figure materialized from behind a thicket of willows bordering the lake. His form was an ominous silhouette against the dappled sunlight.

"Excuse me, can I help—" Cassie's words lodged in her throat as she stumbled to a halt, her sneakers scuffing the gravel. The man stood motionless, his features obscured by the shadow of the hood. There was something eerie about the way he held himself—a stillness that was predatory, a quietude that screamed warning.

"Stay back," she said, her voice firmer than she felt. Cassie took a step backward, prepared to haul ass through the woods if she had to. "I'll scream."

Without warning, the man lunged forward. He was faster than Cassie anticipated, his movements almost a blur. She tried to dodge, but he was upon her in an instant, one hand gripping her shoulder like a vise while the other jabbed something sharp into the tender flesh at the base of her neck.

"Wha—?" Cassie gasped, her eyes widening in shock. The sting of the injection was instantaneous, a fiery lance of pain that scrambled her senses. She wanted to push him away, to flee, but her limbs were becoming uncooperative, heavy as lead.

"Shh, it's just a little pinch," the man whispered, his breath hot against her ear. His voice was a chilling caress, a stark contrast to the agony that began to cascade down her spine, sending out ripples of torment.

As the toxin coursed through her veins, Cassie felt her world tilt, her vision swimming into a kaleidoscope of colors. Trees merged with the sky, the ground swayed beneath her feet, and it all became a swirling abyss.

"Help," she tried to shout, but the sound came out as a feeble croak, lost amidst the cacophony of her disintegrating consciousness. Her thoughts were splintering, shattering under the weight of the poison that invaded her system. Still, she did her best to focus, to pay attention to every detail.

The man's face remained hidden, his identity cloaked in shadow and mystery, but she fought to memorize the outline of his stature, the timbre of his voice—anything that might later serve as a clue.

Her knees buckled, and she reached out desperately, her fingers grazing the rough bark of a tree near the water's edge. It was an anchor in the tempest, a lifeline as reality slipped further and further away. Her grip on the tree loosened, her strength ebbing away as her consciousness waned, leaving her teetering on the precipice of oblivion.

The hooded figure leaned closer, his breath a foul draft on her face. It was hard to know for certain, but she was quite sure he was pulling deeper into the forest. His hands, gloved in darkness, remained steady, expectant. Even as her vision swam and her senses dulled, she could feel the intensity of his gaze upon her.

"Beautiful, just like a pearl," he said, his tone disturbingly reverent.

Cassie's heart plummeted as his words unwound a gruesome tapestry of implications. She knew, with a gut-wrenching certainty, who stood before her now. This was no random mugging, no chance encounter gone awry. The man looming over her, his presence a harbinger of death, was the same one who had claimed four lives before hers—the serial killer who had plunged their community into terror.

So this was it, she realized. Her jog by the lake, the peaceful solitude—it had all been a prelude to becoming another of his victims. Panic clawed at her insides, a wild animal trapped in the snare of inevitability.

"You understand, don't you?" he continued, his voice a hypnotic drawl. "Pain elevates us. It strips away the mundane and reveals the extraordinary. Pressure…like a pearl."

The world was slipping away from Cassie, colors and sounds merging into an indistinct haze. The lake, once a serene mirror reflecting the sky's moods, now wavered in her vision, a watercolor painting caught in the rain. Her limbs felt heavy, unresponsive as he carried her along to some unknown place.

CHAPTER TWENTY THREE

Tessa sat stiffly in a utilitarian chair in a conference room back at the field office, her posture betraying the tension that knotted her shoulders. Jake sat across from her, leaning back in his own seat, eyes unfocused as he tapped a pen against his notepad rhythmically—a metronome to the waiting. There was an electric feeling in the room, the tension of the moment so thick that Tessa could feel it.

Tessa's eyes kept trailing to the door, waiting for the news. They'd left the precinct an hour ago, leaving the crimes that Crabtree and Miller had committed together to the police. Neither would be released any time soon, but for now, Tessa didn't see either of them as being pivotal to the case.

"You know about a watched pot, right?" Jake asked.

"I know," Tessa said, looking away from the door. "This is driving me crazy."

"Same here. And you know what else is driving me crazy?"

"What?" Tessa asked.

"David Benson's fingerprint on that pearl from Edith Harper's house. Even if this new guy turns out to be the killer, we still have no idea how that fits in."

While Tessa had not forgotten about Benson, she did wonder how he was holding up. He, like Crabtree and Miller, was also still being held under suspicion.

"All questions that will hopefully be answered sooner rather than later," he said.

Tessa's phone vibrated against the tabletop, slicing through the monotony. The screen lit up with an incoming text, head with Elle's name. Tessa felt a small spark of comfort. Elle had been her rock, her mentor, for such a long time. She wondered how different this case might be if Elle was here in Portland rather than D.C.

The text was simple and to the point. It read: *Have you kicked that case in the ass yet?*

Frowning, she responded back with: *It's sort of still the other way around. A possible break though…*

She sighed heavily as she set her phone back down, fighting off the dregs of exhaustion.

"Everything okay?" Jake asked.

"Yeah. That was Elle, just checking in."

"You told her about this case?" he asked, surprised.

"Yeah. I…well, I sometimes vent to her about things that are bothering me."

Jake nodded, and she noted the look of slight disappointment on his face. Maybe, Tessa thought, because he'd like to eventually land that role.

"Good to have someone watching your back," he commented, though his expression suggested he understood the complexities tangled within that relationship.

As Tessa looked back to the door, she felt herself pulled by a current towards Sarah. Sarah, who had vanished without a trace, leaving behind a void no amount of resolve could fill. The memory was an old wound that refused to heal, a shadow that stretched across every case, every lead, every dead end.

Sitting at the table, the memory came at her with the speed of a bullet. It was the memory of a morning long past, a morning when the world had tipped on its axis and thrown her life into perpetual disarray.

The empty bed, the sheets still messy and askew. An eighteen-year-old Tessa, just three months from graduating from high school, looking into her sister's bedroom. She'd called out for Sarah, figuring she'd just woken up early and made her way to the bathroom or kitchen. Tessa stood in the doorway, still studying the oddly empty room. She always woke Sarah up in the morning, their father having left for work a full half an hour before either of his daughters woke up to get ready for school.

There was no answer when she called again, louder and with panic in her voice this time. There was only the echo of her own fear rebounding off the walls. Her gaze had caught on the window, the screen pried away from the outside with what might have been hasty desperation or insidious intent. And the window was opened just a bit, stuck in the frame at that last inch or two. A breeze toyed with the edges of the curtains, reaching its fingers into the room as if searching for something long gone.

"Tessa?"

She blinked the memory away, embarrassed to have slid so easily into it. She looked up and saw that the door to the room had finally opened. An agent she knew only moderately well—an older agent named Wendy Hopkins—stood just inside the doorway with a smartpad in her hand.

"Sorry. Zoned out," Tessa said. "Do we have it?"

"We have it," Hopkins said. "The credit card transaction led us to an address here in the city. Less than twenty miles from here."

"An address?" Tessa repeated, her pulse quickening. This was tangible, a concrete step forward after wading through uncertainty. The possibility of confronting the man from Crabtree's records surged through her, a tide of anticipation laced with the bitter tang of old fears.

"Is it solid?" Jake asked, mirroring Tessa's mix of elation and skepticism.

"Looks like it," the agent affirmed. "Came up under a name with a pretty nasty history. Domestic abuse, public indecency, assault. You need an assist?"

"I think we're good, but thanks," Jake said, already getting to his feet. "Damned good work, Hopkins. Thanks."

Tessa nodded in agreement, her mind racing. Every lead had the potential to unravel at the seams, but this one felt different. A match. An address to perhaps the strongest, most likely suspect of all. A flicker of possibility in the darkness. For the first time in a long while, the hunt seemed to gain momentum, and Tessa was ready to chase it to the end.

They moved in tandem, leaving the conference room and passing cubicles where agents typed or spoke in hushed tones, the rhythm of their investigation syncing with the cadence of their steps. Each footstep seemed to resonate with the possibility that they were moments away from confronting the enigmatic man who had eluded them for so long.

"Wouldn't it be something? If after all this—" Jake started.

"Don't jinx it," she cut in, her voice tinged with a playful severity. Superstition wasn't part of their toolkit, but old habits died hard.

"Right," Jake conceded. His eyes were stern as they hurried for the exit. Oddly enough, the bruise on his jaw seemed to fit the moment, and Tessa found herself reminded of just how handsome he could be.

"Let's just focus on what's next," she said, re-orienting her own mind. "The address, the approach, how we're going to handle it," Tessa said, marshaling her thoughts, her years of training kicking in to suppress the flood of emotion threatening to surface. "One step at a time."

"Agreed," Jake nodded, his gaze sharpening as they approached the exit.

The doors parted before them, the late afternoon sun spilling across the threshold, painting everything in a golden hue. Tessa squinted into the light, the brightness a stark contrast to the darkness she expected just beyond the horizon.

CHAPTER TWENTY FOUR

The sedan’s wheels crunched over old, dusty gravel as Jake pulled up to the curb. Tessa peered through the windshield at the house their address had led them to. It looked like a relic from a bygone era, its paint peeling and shutters hanging askew. It was located on a strip of tree-shrouded two-lane road where multiple houses that looked similar were hidden away from the city but just close enough to feel its shadow. Tessa could feel the weight of anticipation in her chest—a heavy, slow thud that matched the ticking of the car's cooling engine.

The only clear sign of habitation was the old pickup truck parked in the driveway.

They both exited the vehicle, the slam of the doors louder than they would have liked in the stillness of the rural landscape. As they approached the house, Tessa peered in through the passenger side window of the truck.

“Jake, have a look at this.”

Jake came over, looking through the window to see what had caught Tessa’s attention. It was a crumpled-up uniform—the sort that might be worn by the employee of a landscaping or maintenance company. It was. clue form earlier in the case, coming back to haunt them.

“This feels right,” Jake said, sounding hopeful and on edge.

“I think so, too.”

They quietly approached the front door, Tessa not quite sure what to expect. Jake took the lead, raising his hands to knock. But before he did, door, a low sound stopped them in their tracks.

A muffled moan, barely perceptible, but undeniably human.

"Did you hear that?" Tessa whispered, her hand instinctively reaching for her service weapon.

"Someone's inside," Jake replied, his voice tight with urgency.

Now with a heightened feel for things, Tessa quickly dissected the moment and understood what the smartest play would be. They had a potential victim inside, someone possibly hurt. And maybe even the killer.

"Split up?" she suggested.

"Good call. I'll take the front. You circle around to the back."

"Be careful," she said, locking eyes with him, reading the same determination mirrored back at her.

Tessa moved stealthily off the ragged porch, heading to the side of the house. Her senses heightened with every step. The overgrown backyard was a tangle of weeds and brambles that clawed at her pants. She cursed silently, her frustration growing. This untended jungle was mostly dead. The shell of an old riding lawn mower was parked dead and useless next to a narrow back porch. The porch wasn't in much better shape than the mower, the rails lopsided and the wooden stairs cracked.

Tessa quietly climbed the porch stairs and found the back door unlocked. Her pulse quickened, her mind flashing through possible scenarios—was their suspect so confident he didn't bother with locks? Or was he far enough away from the city that he didn't find it necessary?

Or was this a trap?

Tessa drew her Glock and pushed the door open with the heel of her boot. The interior was dim, the air stale, filled with the scent of mildew and neglect. Tessa's eyes adjusted slowly as she stepped inside, alert for any sign of movement. The back door opened into the kitchen. It was basic and quite dirty. A pan sat on the stove. An empty package of noodles sat on the counter.

Her thoughts raced. If the killer was there, each second counted. And if the moan they'd heard was a victim, then time was equally an enemy. She had to find the source of that sound, had to ensure no more lives were taken by this monster they were hunting.

Tessa's footsteps were silent as she exited the kitchen. To her right, he saw Jake expertly clearing the front room. She did the same, turning to her left and investigating the hallway. She cleared each room methodically: a small bathroom, a bedroom containing only a bed and an old, tattered bureau. A grimy window looked out onto the untended backyard.

She stepped back out into the hallway and came to the last room on the right—another bedroom. The air in the room was still, as if it had been trapped there for years, waiting for this moment. Dust danced in the slivers of light that fought their way through the boarded-up windows, and Tessa felt the weight of each particle as she stepped forward. To the back of the room, a door opened up on what she thought was the entrance to a basement. She started in that direction, but as she did, her eyes scanned the walls.

He paused, her heart quickening. The wall was adorned with photographs—snapshots of ordinary homes at dusk, each carrying an eerie sense of foreboding.

"God…" Tessa muttered under her breath.

The houses were all familiar. They were all the homes of the victims. Each was a silent testament to the horrors that had befallen within.

This is it, she thought. *We found his lair…*

Beneath the pictures, on a makeshift shelf, lay trinkets: a woman's hairbrush with strands still entwined, a wristwatch…and pearls. There were two necklaces and a few individual pearls sitting to the side.

She nearly went back into the house to get Jake. She knew that calling out to him would be foolish; if the killer was here, she'd be giving away her position. She turned to head back into the hallway when the sound reached her ears again.

A moan. A woman, she was quite sure. It wasn't necessarily a moan of pain. It was more of a groggy sound, like someone fighting to come awake. And it was coming from the door behind her—from down in the darkness of what she thought was a basement.

She steadied her breath and moved towards it, the hardwood floor groaning beneath her boots like an ominous prelude.

"Hello?" Her voice was firm but softened by empathy. "FBI."

She made her way down a narrow, creaking staircase. A single dangling bulb hung from the ceiling ahead, revealing a partially finished basement. The floor was concrete and a few walls had been put up but not finalized.

As she planted her feet on the concrete, she realized the air was thicker here. Tessa's senses were heightened; every shadow seemed alive, every whisper of wind a potential threat. But her focus was unbreakable, honed by years of training—she followed the sound with the precision of a hawk tracking prey.

Turning a corner on her right, alongside one of the partially completed walls, her eyes landed on a figure huddled at the back corner. A young woman…very much alive. She was dressed in basic attire—a black shirt and shorts. And there was a string of pearls around her neck. She looked only barely conscious, making Tessa think of the pin-prick injection marks on all of the victims.

A wave of relief washed over Tessa, momentarily warming the chill that had settled in her bones. The woman before her was bound, her eyes fluttering open wider by the moment.

"Hey, it's okay, it's okay," Tessa said as she hurried toward the woman. Approaching with, "You're going to be fine. I'm here now."

She knelt beside the petrified woman, who flinched at her touch before recognizing the intent behind it. Tessa's fingers worked quickly and deftly at the ropes binding the woman's arms behind her back.,

"Can you stand?" Tessa asked, supporting her with a steady arm.

The woman nodded weakly, a tear carving a path down her dirt-streaked face.

"Good." Tessa's mind raced as she plotted their exit strategy. "We're going to walk out of here together. Stay close to me."

Tessa's muscles tensed, ready to hoist the trembling victim to her feet when a shadow flickered at the periphery of her vision. She turned, instincts flaring, and she saw another figure. For a confusing moment, she was sure it was just Jake. He'd found the basement and had come down to assist.

But the man standing at the start of the wall, just five feet away, was not Jake. It was a hulking silhouette against the dim light, sending a ripple of ice through Tessa's veins.

Tessa gently lowered the woman back to the floor, doing her best to keep her Glock trained on the man.

“I'm with the FBI,” Tessa said. “Don't mo—”

But he was already charging forward, his movements a blur. Tessa's training kicked in; she parried a strike, pivoted, and struck back. Each blow she landed was precise, meant to disable, but he was relentless. She didn't want to shoot unless she absolutely had to, and for now, it seemed that she could handle him without such extreme measures. Plus, with the Glock held in her hand, her right-handed jabs carried more impact.

The dance was deadly, each step fraught with danger. Tessa felt the rhythm of her heart pounding, the tightness in her lungs, the adrenaline fueling her defiance. The killer managed two strikes—one to her ribs and another to her collarbones. Each one was cataloged away, her body refusing to acknowledge pain, only the need to survive, to fight.

Then, with one hurricane-like movement, Tessa wheeled herself around and placed all of her weight into her forearms. She caught the killer and slammed him hard against the wall. It cracked and dented behind him, plaster raining down.

The killer's right hand came up as if in a defensive motion. But that wasn't what he was doing at all. And Tessa didn't understand this until it was too late.

A swift prick pressure at her neck so subtle she might've imagined it if not for the immediate wash of dizziness that followed. No pain, but an unmistakable betrayal by her own body. Her knees buckled, the world tilted violently.

"Got you," the killer hissed triumphantly, like a kid playing tag.

Tessa tried to fight it, every fiber straining to stay awake, stay alive. Her thoughts became disjointed, desperate.

As unconsciousness wrapped its cold fingers around her, her last coherent thought was a vow—an oath to the victim and to herself.

Not over... she thought. *Have to...stop...you...*

And with that defiant promise still burning in the recesses of her mind, Tessa felt herself being slowly swallowed by the void.

CHAPTER TWENTY FIVE

The cold, hard floor beneath her offered no comfort as Tessa's consciousness flickered like a faulty light bulb. Her vision blurred and sharpened intermittently, the dimly lit basement morphing in and out of focus. The musty air was thick with the scent of old dust and lingering fear. She tried to move, but her limbs were leaden, unresponsive. It was as if her body had been divorced from her brain, leaving her frustratingly immobile.

Her thoughts were sluggish, but she clung to one hope – that the killer remained unaware that Jake was somewhere above them, silent and unseen. And beyond that hope was a question: why had the killer brought this latest victim here, to his lair? What was different about this one?

As a glimmer of clarity pierced her haze of confusion, Tessa was oddly grateful for the numbness that usually frustrated her. She was well aware that her inability to feel pain might be making the drug she'd been injected with a bit less impactful. It might very well be the very thing keeping her mind from succumbing completely to the darkness. That small blessing could be what stood between life and death right now.

"Pretty thing, isn't it?" The killer's voice slithered into her ears, oily and smooth. Tessa's gaze struggled to settle on his face as he loomed over her, a smirk twisting his lips. He dangled a string of pearls before her eyes, each bead glinting like a moon in the weak light before he gently laid it upon her neck.

"Like a queen," he sneered, fingers lingering at her throat just a second too long. "Your friend Cassie was meant to wear these." His taunt was a jagged blade cutting through her foggy mind. "But I'll return them to her as soon as I have you out of the way."

Tessa felt a frisson of horror mixed with revulsion. He knew the would-be victim's name. He'd done his research like the others. But still, the question nagged at Tessa.

Why did he bring her here?

"Cassie's grandmother was the one I wanted," he said. "She'd been on my list from the start. But she passed away two weeks ago and

I…well, I had to make other plans. You see, because grandma kicked the bucket, dear Cassie came into millions. Oh, how quickly they forget their elders when money sings its siren song. But I... I didn't forget. No, I simply adjusted my plan."

Tessa's heart pounded in her chest, the sound roaring in her ears. Rage simmered within her, igniting a will to fight she thought had been extinguished by the drugs coursing through her veins. If she could just keep him talking, if she could just hold onto consciousness a little longer...

"Tell me," she rasped, her voice barely audible, "How did you get close to them?"

He paused, cocking his head to the side as if considering whether to indulge her curiosity. Or maybe he was surprised by just how coherent she could be while under the haze of his drug. The sadistic pleasure in his eyes told her he relished this game of cat and mouse. And Tessa, despite the encroaching shadows at the edge of her vision, realized this was the only game she had left to play.

The taste of copper flooded Tessa's mouth, a biting reminder of her vulnerability. She was trapped in a macabre tableau, a damsel not just in distress but in the clutches of a monster. Her mind, foggy and fragmented from the toxin, grappled for clarity.

"Your... methods," she managed to choke out. "How did you... get so close?" Her voice was a mere ghost of its former strength, but it was all she could muster to keep him engaged.

He smiled proudly. "I am a chameleon of sorts. I become what they need—repairman, delivery guy, concerned neighbor. And because they all think themselves so high and mighty above those in simple, labor-heavy unfirms, it was so easy. It's amazing how a uniform can render you invisible in such communities."

Invisible. The word echoed in Tessa's head. Jake needed to stay that way just a little longer. She curled her fingers, begging for them to respond. A surge of panic rose when they didn't obey. The darkness at the periphery of her vision crept closer, threatening to engulf her.

And then, as if summoned by her silent plea, she saw his shape step into view behind the killer. Stealthy and quiet, Tessa's own private angel. His presence was a jolt to her system, a spark reigniting her will to survive.

"FBI! Drop it!" Jake's command was a thunderclap in the oppressive silence.

The killer whirled around, startled, his eyes widening at the sight of Jake. In that split second, Tessa saw an opportunity—a sliver of hope. But as quickly as it appeared, it vanished into chaos.

The killer charged, and Jake fired off a shot from his drawn Glock. He aimed low, hoping to just maim the man, but he went *too* low and the shot missed. There was not enough time to fire off a second shot before the men collided with the ferocity of a storm, a tangle of limbs and raw survival instinct. The sound of flesh against flesh, grunts, and curses filled the room. Tessa tried to will her body to move, to do something, anything, but she was a prisoner within her own flesh, forced to watch the struggle unfold.

Jake mimicked Tessa's earlier attack by slamming the killer into the wall. But the killer rebounded right away, and they slammed together again. Jake threw a right-handed haymaker that just barely landed, while the killer drove his knee into Jake's stomach.

A gunshot shattered the tension, the report ringing off the concrete walls. Tessa flinched, a thread of relief weaving through her terror as she saw the killer stagger back, a dark stain blooming on his shirt.

But the triumph was short-lived. With a savage countermovement, the killer lunged in a final act of desperation, sending Jake crashing to the ground. Tessa heard the sickening thud of skull against concrete—a sound she was sure would haunt her nightmares if she lived through this night.

"Jake…" She tried to scream it, but the drug caused it to sound like little more than a whisper. She was drained, tired, so close to the darkness now.

She watched helplessly, her consciousness ebbing away as blood trickled from Jake's head, pooling beneath him in a stark crimson halo. The killer loomed over her once more, his shadow a dark omen. Despair clawed at her chest, and her vision tunneled to a single point of light.

But even as she fought against the encroaching darkness, she knew she was losing. Her eyelids drooped heavily as she fought to stay present, to remain in the fight she knew she was losing. The killer's face swam into her blurred vision, an eerie smile playing on his lips as he leaned close, the heat of his breath a sickening caress against her cheek.

"You thought you could stop me," he sneered, his voice a serpentine hiss that slithered into her ear. "But you're nothing—just another victim. You weren't on my list…not in my plans. But I'll enjoy this all the same."

He grabbed at the pearl necklace he'd draped around her neck. With a sudden jerk, he looped and drew them tight. Despite the absence of pain, she understood the danger of this as her air supply was cut off. His strength was insane, given that he'd just been shot. She gasped for air, her fingers trying to claw at the constricting band, but her limbs were treacherous in their sluggishness.

Tessa's vision dimmed further, the edges of her world curling into darkness. But as she teetered on the brink of unconsciousness, a loud crack shattered the silence. Another gunshot.

The pressure around her neck vanished as the killer stumbled backward, his eyes wide with shock. A crimson flower bloomed on the side of his head, and he slid down the wall, leaving a smudged trail of red.

Her lungs screamed for air, gulping down precious oxygen as she looked around frantically. And there, amidst the chaos, stood Cassie, her hand trembling, holding Tessa's Glock with smoke whispering from its barrel.

The young woman's eyes met hers, fierce and unyielding despite the tears that streamed down her face. There was rage and anger there, but beyond all of that, there was something broken that might never be fixed again. She'd had the wherewithal to pretend to still be tied up, to be completely shocked and out of it…and she'd taken her chance.

"I couldn't let him... couldn't," Cassie stammered, lowering the gun to her side. She then threw it to the ground and if she'd suddenly started to find it revolting.

As warmth seeped back into Tessa's limbs, her control over them remained elusive. The world spun, an unfocused carousel of shadows and murmurs. Time slowed, each second stretching out as reality flickered like a faulty lightbulb.

"Thank you," Tessa whispered the words an anchor in the storm. Her head lolled to the side, the last vestiges of strength fleeing her body as the darkness claimed her. But before surrendering completely, she was swallowed up while seeing one last hopeful moment.

Jake was stirring, getting groggily into a crawling position. Blood was trailing down the left side of his face. He was hurt, but he was alive.

And with that, Tessa succumbed to the void, her spirit content in the knowledge that justice had, at last, been served—delivered by hands once bound by fear, now freed by courage.

CHAPTER TWENTY SIX

Consciousness crept back to Tessa with the subtlety of a whisper in a thunderstorm. Her eyes fluttered open to the sterile white blur of an ambulance ceiling, the siren's wail distant, as if she was underwater. The world rocked gently beneath her, and she felt as if she were trapped somewhere between wakefulness and sleep.

"Jake... Cassie..." Her voice was a rasp, each syllable a struggle that clawed its way out of her throat.

The paramedic, a young woman with compassionate eyes, turned to her with a reassuring smile. "They're fine, Agent Flint. Cassie is with another team, and Agent Sullivan…well, he was a bit more stubborn. He may have a concussion, but he wanted to make sure you were okay before he'd agree to be treated.

"Sounds about right," she murmured.

Tessa's thoughts were sluggish, like trying to run through knee-deep mud. Jake had taken a hard hit; the image of his head leaking blood on the concrete floor flashed before her eyes, mingling with the terror of the strangling pearls.

"Try to relax," the paramedic suggested, checking the monitor beside her. "We'll get you to the hospital soon. You should try to sleep if you can."

Sleep—the word alone was a sedative. She had been running on empty for days, and her body pushed past its limit in pursuit of a killer who was now just a lifeless husk in a cold basement. Her eyelids grew heavy, succumbing to exhaustion's sweet lull. As slumber wrapped around her, Tessa surrendered.

Asleep, she was only vaguely aware of the ambulance doors opening at some point, followed by the rush of movement as she was wheeled into the hospital. More lights, more voices. But why? She'd not been seriously hurt. Injected with something…strangled a bit. But she was fine. Right?

Hospital corridors passed in a blur, the fluorescent lights above streaking across her vision like shooting stars. She was aware of voices, brisk and professional, discussing her vitals, the drug coursing through her veins, the non-lethal verdict that kept panic at bay. It was all distant background noise to the sound she truly longed for—the one voice that mattered.

"Hey, Tess."

It was Jake, his voice a gentle drawl. He was there, beside her bed, his presence a beacon in the hazy fog of her mind. His hand found hers, warmth seeping into her chilled fingers. It took his presence for her to understand that not only had she gotten some sleep, she'd slept *hard.*

"Jake..." Her own relief was palpable, a silent tide washing over her. "How are you?"

"They thought I had a concussion but I was cleared." He pointed to an unsightly bandage on the side of his head and smirked. "Eleven stitches, though. So….hooray."

"Why am I even here?" she asked, her voice still cracking.

"They weren't sure what you'd been injected with. They're giving Cassie Baylor—the intended fifth victim—the same treatment. It's the same drug…well, the same one the killer used on the other victims."

She nodded and opened her mouth to say something else. But Jake gave her hand a squeeze as he shook his head.

"Get some rest," he said. "I'll be right here."

And with those words, she did manage to fall back into sleep. She Tessa drifted deeper into the darkness, her last conscious thought a flicker of Sarah. That undying ember of loss and longing nestled deep within her heart, bringing both grief and comfort.

***

Tessa sat on the edge of the examination bed, legs dangling. The incessant beeping of the heart monitor next to her served as an odd lullaby—a reminder that she was still among the living.

"Your vitals are stable, Agent Flint," Dr. Patel announced, entering the room with a clipboard in hand. He'd been I an out of her room ever since she'd stirred awake an hour ago and she was ready to get out of there.. "The lab confirmed the substance you were injected with is non-lethal. A dirty little cocktail for sure, but you'll be fine. As will Ms. Baylor."

Tessa nodded, processing the information. The absence of lethality did little to ease the memory of the drug coursing through her veins, the way she'd had no control over her body.

"Can I go home?" Her voice was hoarse, but the resolve behind it was as solid as the determination that had driven her throughout this case.

"Yes, we're discharging you. But you need to rest, and someone should stay with you for the next twenty-four hours." He offered her a small, understanding smile.

"Understood," Tessa replied, swinging her legs off the bed and rising to her feet. She felt the steadiness return to her stance, the familiar weight of her own strength anchoring her to the moment.

Dr. Patel handed her a smart pad with a discharge form already pulled up. She took it, her hands steady despite the ordeal of it all. She filled it out as quickly as she could and then left the room and then the hall, heading for the elevators. She pulled out her phone to call for an Uber, but stopped short of doing so when she came to the elevators.

Jake was standing there, hands in his pockets, waiting. "So they're letting you go?"

"Yeah. I'm fine."

"Need a ride home?"

"No. I'll Uber to my car at the office and—"

"Nope. I know they've asked you to rest. I'm taking you home, and we'll figure out the car situation tomorrow."

Tessa chuckled. "Yeah…despite all the sleep I just got, I was told to rest."

"You didn't sleep as long as you think," he said as they stepped onto the elevator. "It's only 11:30. You've only been here for six hours."

The hell of it was that as they took the elevators down, Tessa realized that she did feel sleepy. Two days of no sleep and a cocktail designed to incapacitate would do that to you, she supposed. And as she stepped out of the halo of the hospital lights and into the darkened parking lot, she found that she was looking *very* forward to crawling into her own bed.

They made their way to Jake's car, and as soon as it started moving, Tessa thought she might fall asleep again.

"Talk to me," she said. "Keep me from falling asleep."

"You sure?"

"Yes."

"Well, I found out a few hours ago that the police found out why David Benson's prints were on the pearl from Edith Harper's house."

Tessa turned towards him, interest piqued. "How?"

"Turns out Benson bumped into our killer—named Cameron Johnson, by the way—earlier that day," Jake explained, navigating the car onto the highway. " Johnson worked for a landscaping company that is employed by at least four different communities around the city.

He happened to see Benson in a convenience store parking lot and played it like he'd just found the pearl lying around. Made a big show of it, according to Benson. Johnson asked Benson to take a look...asked if he knew what it was."

"Just a ruse to get his prints on it?" Tessa speculated.

"That's what everyone is assuming."

"Smart," Tessa muttered, leaning back against the seat, her mind racing. It was a clever trick, one that spoke volumes about Cameron Johnson's cunning nature. The web of deceit was intricate, woven with precision—a deadly game of predator and prey where the stakes were life itself. She was glad they'd put an end to his evil.

"Too smart," Jake agreed, his gaze steady on the road ahead. "It almost worked."

When they arrived at her house just past midnight, the familiar sight was both comforting and jarring—an oasis of normalcy amidst the storm of their recent ordeal. Jake parked the car and turned to face her, his expression softening.

"Would you like me to come in for a bit?" he offered gently. "Aren't you supposed to have someone looking after you?

"What are you, my nurse?" she joked.

"If you want."

Tessa considered the offer, fatigue warring with the desire for companionship. She shook her head finally, her voice softer than she intended. "I appreciate it, Jake, but I just want to crash. You understand, right?"

"Of course," he replied, his voice laced with an understanding that went beyond the words. "but you'll call if you need anything, right?"

"I promise." As she opened the door, his hand brushed against hers—a fleeting touch that sent a current through her weary body.

"Get some rest, Tessa," he said, his eyes holding hers in a moment that stretched into something charged with possibility.

"Thanks, Jake. For everything," she said and stepped out into the cool night air. Watching his car drive away, she felt a pang of something akin to longing—her heart whispering of roads not yet taken.

She walked inside tot eh chorus of crashing waves from the sea behind the house, the door creaking open to welcome her back. In the silence, she could hear the echo of Jake's voice, could almost feel the ghost of his touch. Maybe she should have taken him up on his offer.

She was sure she'd head straight to bed but instead found herself walking to the kitchen. There, she chugged down two glasses of water and threw a sandwich together. As she ate it, she ventured through her bedroom into the adjoined master bathroom. She ran a hot tub of water, leaning listlessly against the sink as she waited for it to fill.

Moments later, she sank into the tub and felt like she was melting. She listened to the waves outside and the dripping of the faucet. Steam curled up around her, fogging the mirror and creating an ethereal atmosphere that felt worlds away from the violence and chaos she'd just experienced. Her muscles relaxed beneath the heat, the tension seeping out of her.

"Sarah," she whispered to the silence, the name slipping out like a prayer or a curse. The surface of the water shivered as she exhaled, ripples distorting her reflection. Sarah, with her unfathomable disappearance, and the endless string of mysteries behind her. It had all left a void in Tessa's life—a mystery that gnawed at her, demanding attention.

"Where are you?" The question was meant for the absent sister but echoed back to Tessa herself. Where was she in this labyrinth of crime and pain? Had she lost herself chasing shadows, or had it made her sharper, more resolved?

She submerged herself completely, letting the water fill her ears until all she could hear was the sound of her own heartbeat, steady and determined. As she broke the surface again, gasping for air, the clarity of purpose filled her lungs just as surely as oxygen.

Toweling off, Tessa stood naked before the steamed mirror, wiping away the condensation to reveal her own steel-blue eyes staring back at her. They held a glint that hadn't been there before—hardened by what she'd endured, yet brighter with the flame of justice that refused to be extinguished.

She wrapped the towel around herself, feeling the fabric catch on the rough edges of her determination. Moving to the bedroom, she pulled on a set of comfortable clothes, each movement deliberate, each thought honing the edge of her resolve.

Maye, not tomorrow…but sometime soon, she was going to request a meeting with Lawson and request that Sarah's case be opened again. Because he was beginning to understand that if there was no solid end to that particular mystery, she'd never truly have peace.

She'd rather have a sad, heart-breaking answer than no answer at all.

Sarah's disappearance was no mere footnote in her life—it was the prologue to the person she'd become, an agent who would stop at nothing to uncover the truth.

With that decision made, Tessa switched off the lamp, allowing darkness to envelop her. In its embrace, she found a strange comfort. After all, it was in darkness that her commitment shone brightest, unwavering and fierce.

NOW AVAILABLE!

BARELY HEARD
(A Tessa Flint FBI Suspense Thriller—Book 2)

When victims of a new serial killer are found adorned with a mysterious snowflake pendant, FBI Agent Tessa Flint must navigate the frozen depths of this sadistic killer's mind to save the next one in time—and to save herself…

"Molly Black has written a taut thriller that will keep you on the edge of your seat… I absolutely loved this book and can't wait to read the next book in the series!"
—Reader review for Girl One: Murder

BARELY HEARD is BOOK #2 of a brand-new series by critically acclaimed and #1 bestselling mystery and suspense author Molly Black, whose books have received over 2,000 five-star reviews and ratings. The series begins with BARELY SEEN (book #1).

The Tessa Flint series is an intense and riveting crime thriller that centers around a captivating and deeply troubled female protagonist. This gripping mystery series is filled with constant action, suspense, unexpected surprises, shocking discoveries, and propelled by a relentless speed that will have you engrossed in the story long into the night. Fans of Lisa Gardner, Teresa Driscoll and Karin Slaughter are sure to fall in love.

Future books in the series are also available.

"I binge read this book. It hooked me in and didn't stop till the last few pages… I look forward to reading more!"
—Reader review for Found You

“I loved this book! Fast-paced plot, great characters and interesting insights into investigating cold cases. I can't wait to read the next book!”
—Reader review for Girl One: Murder

“Very good book… You will feel like you are right there looking for the kidnapper! I know I will be reading more in this series!”
—Reader review for Girl One: Murder

“This is a very well written book and holds your interest from page 1… Definitely looking forward to reading the next one in the series, and hopefully others as well!”
—Reader review for Girl One: Murder

“Wow, I cannot wait for the next in this series. Starts with a bang and just keeps going.”
—Reader review for Girl One: Murder

“Well written book with a great plot, one that will keep you up at night. A page turner!”
—Reader review for Girl One: Murder

“A great suspense that keeps you reading… can't wait for the next in this series!”
—Reader review for Found You

“Sooo soo good! There are a few unforeseen twists… I binge read this like I binge watch Netflix. It just sucks you in.”
—Reader review for Found You

Molly Black

Bestselling author Molly Black is author of the MAYA GRAY FBI suspense thriller series, comprising eleven books; of the RYLIE WOLF FBI suspense thriller series, comprising six books; of the TAYLOR SAGE FBI suspense thriller series, comprising eight books; of the KATIE WINTER FBI suspense thriller series, comprising eleven books (and counting); of the RUBY HUNTER FBI suspense thriller series, comprising five books (and counting); of the CAITLIN DARE FBI suspense thriller series, comprising six books (and counting); of the REESE LINK mystery series, comprising six books (and counting); of the CLAIRE KING FBI suspense thriller series, comprising seven books (and counting); of the PIPER WOODS mystery series, comprising six books (and counting); of the GRACE FORD mystery series, comprising seven books (and counting); of the CASEY BOLT mystery series, comprising five books (and counting); of the JADE SAVAGE mystery series, comprising five books (and counting); of the TESSA FLINT mystery series, comprising seven books (and counting); of the CLARA PIKE FBI thriller series, comprising five books (and counting); and of the ELISE CLOSE psychological thriller series, comprising five books (and counting).

An avid reader and lifelong fan of the mystery and thriller genres, Molly loves to hear from you, so please feel free to visit www.mollyblackauthor.com to learn more and stay in touch.

BOOKS BY MOLLY BLACK

ELISE CLOSE MYSTERY SERIES
BEHIND HER LIES (Book #1)
BEHIND HER SMILE (Book #2)
BEHIND HER SECRETS (Book #3)
BEHIND HER GATES (Book #4)
BEHIND LOCKED DOORS (Book #5)

CLARA PIKE FBI SUSPENSE THRILLER SERIES
REMEMBER THE FEAR (Book #1)
REMEMBER THE DEAD (Book #2)
REMEMBER THE LIES (Book #3)
REMEMBER THE SILENCE (Book #4)
REMEMBER THE PAST (Book #5)

PIPER WOODS FBI SUSPENSE THRILLER
SOMEWHERE SAFE (Book #1)
SOMEWHERE SANE (Book #2)
SOMEWHERE WHOLE (Book #3)
SOMEWHERE FAR (Book #4)
SOMEWHERE WRONG (Book #5)
SOMEWHERE HIDDEN (Book #6)

TESSA FLINT MYSTERY SERIES
BARELY SEEN (Book #1)
BARELY HEARD (Book #2)
BARELY FORGOTTEN (Book #3)
BARELY MISSING (Book #4)
BARELY ALIVE (Book #5)
BARELY THERE (Book #6)
BARELY SILENT (Book #7)

CASEY BOLT MYSTERY SERIES
BROKEN (Book #1)
FLAWED (Book #2)

BLEMISHED (Book #3)
DAMAGED (Book #4)
TWISTED (Book #5)

GRACE FORD MYSTERY SERIES
NEARLY MINE (Book #1)
NEARLY SAFE (Book #2)
NEARLY FREE (Book #3)
NEARLY GONE (Book #4)
NEARLY HIS (Book #5)

CLAIRE KING MYSTERY SERIES
ONCE HE SEES (Book #1)
ONCE HE LONGS (Book #2)
ONCE HE TAKES (Book #3)
ONCE HE FEELS (Book #4)
ONCE HE KNOWS (Book #5)

MAYA GRAY MYSTERY SERIES
GIRL ONE: MURDER (Book #1)
GIRL TWO: TAKEN (Book #2)
GIRL THREE: TRAPPED (Book #3)
GIRL FOUR: LURED (Book #4)
GIRL FIVE: BOUND (Book #5)
GIRL SIX: FORSAKEN (Book #6)
GIRL SEVEN: CRAVED (Book #7)
GIRL EIGHT: HUNTED (Book #8)
GIRL NINE: GONE (Book #9)
GIRL TEN: WANTED (Book #10)
GIRL ELEVEN: VANISHED (Book #11)

RYLIE WOLF FBI SUSPENSE THRILLER SERIES
FOUND YOU (Book #1)
CAUGHT YOU (Book #2)
SEE YOU (Book #3)
WANT YOU (Book #4)
TAKE YOU (Book #5)
DARE YOU (Book #6)

TAYLOR SAGE FBI SUSPENSE THRILLER SERIES
DON'T LOOK (Book #1)
DON'T BREATHE (Book #2)
DON'T RUN (Book #3)
DON'T FLINCH (Book #4)
DON'T REMEMBER (Book #5)
DON'T TELL (Book #6)

KATIE WINTER FBI SUSPENSE THRILLER SERIES
SAVE ME (Book #1)
REACH ME (Book #2)
HIDE ME (Book #3)
BELIEVE ME (Book #4)
HELP ME (Book #5)
FORGET ME (Book #6)
HOLD ME (Book #7)
PROTECT ME (Book #8)
REMEMBER ME (Book #9)
CATCH ME (Book #10)
WATCH ME (Book #11)

RUBY HUNTER FBI SUSPENSE THRILLER SERIES
IF I RUN (Book #1)
IF I TELL (Book #2)
IF I LIVE (Book #3)
IF I FORGET (Book #4)
IF I RETURN (Book #5)

CAITLIN DARE FBI SUSPENSE THRILLER SERIES
COME GET ME (Book #1)
COME FIND ME (Book #2)
COME TAKE ME (Book #3)
COME CATCH ME (Book #4)
COME SAVE ME (Book #5)

REESE LINK MYSTERY SERIES
BEYOND REASON (Book #1)
BEYOND REACH (Book #2)
BEYOND REPAIR (Book #3)
BEYOND DOUBT (Book #4)

BEYOND NORMAL (Book #5)

Printed in Great Britain
by Amazon

54240838R00089